Young Marian's Adventures in Sherwood Forest

A Girls to the Rescue Novel

BY STEPHEN MOOSER

Meadowbrook Press

Distributed by Simon & Schuster
New York

Library of Congress Cataloging-in-Publication Data:

Mooser, Stephen.
  Young Marian's adventures in Sherwood forest : a girls to the rescue novel / by
Stephen Mooser.
      p. cm.
  Summary: Thirteen-year-old Marian and her friend Robin team up to rescue her
father whom the Sheriff has wrongly condemned to death.
  ISBN 0-88166-277-1 (Meadowbrook).
  ISBN 0-671-57551-1 (Simon & Schuster)
  1. Maid Marian (Legendary character)—Juvenile Fiction. [1. Maid Marian
(Legendary character)—Fiction. 2. Great Britain—History—Richard I, 1189-
1199—Fiction.] I. Title.
  PZ7.M78817Yo 1997
  [Fic]—dc21   96-53114
                                                          CIP
                                                          AC

© 1997 by Stephen Mooser

Published by Meadowbrook Press, 5451 Smetana Drive, Minnetonka, MN 55343

BOOK TRADE DISTRIBUTION by Simon & Schuster, a division of
Simon and Schuster, Inc., 1230 Avenue of the Americas, New York, NY 10020

Editor: Bruce Lansky
Editorial Coordinator: Liya Lev Oertel
Copyeditors: Kate Green, Liya Lev Oertel
Production Manager: Joe Gagne
Production Assistant: Danielle White
Cover Design: Nancy Tuminelly
Cover Illustration: Creative Network: Virginia Kylberg

00 99 98 97   10 9 8 7 6 5 4 3 2 1

Printed in the United States of America

Dedication

This book is for Zoe.

Contents

Introduction

The legend of Robin Hood is more than eight hundred years old. Over the centuries, Robin's exploits have been celebrated in songs, poems, books, and movies. Robin is always portrayed as clever, courageous, and noble—robbing from the rich to give to the poor and rescuing beautiful Maid Marian from the clutches of the evil Sheriff of Nottingham.

I am tired of stories featuring beautiful but helpless damsels in distress who must be rescued by "Prince Charming"—aren't you? That's why I visualized an altogether different treatment of the Robin and Marian story:

Why not pit a spunky thirteen-year-old Marian and her friend Robin of Loxley against the cruel and conniving Sheriff of Nottingham and his thugs? Why not make Marian a clever, courageous, noble hero—just like Robin Hood and just like the other heroes of *Girls to the Rescue* stories?

Stephen Mooser is one of my favorite authors of children's fiction. One of his books, *Elvis Is Back, and He's in the Sixth Grade!*, had me on the edge of my chair and in stitches. Now he's created two exciting, fun heroes—young Marian and Robin—for whom you'll be cheering right up to the final page.

Bruce Lansky

CHAPTER ONE

TWO FOREVER

A cold and cruel wind was blowing. It had sprung up at daybreak, high in the ancient English hills beyond Sherwood Forest. From there it had swept through the wooded passes and across the grassy plains until it reached the mighty castle that loomed above the town of Nottingham. It paused long enough to rattle the castle's dark windows, then dipped over the moat and blew swiftly past the wooden huts clustered below. Finally the wind entered Sherwood Forest where, slowed by the trees and warmed by the rising sun, it was soon transformed into nothing more than a harmless little breeze. It was barely even that, in fact, by the time it reached the large stone estate that a young girl named Maid Marian shared with her father, Geoffrey the Magistrate.

When the breeze found Marian this bright spring morning, she was outside chasing a piglet around the yard. "Timothy! Come back here!" she cried, shaking her finger. "You naughty pig! Stop!"

Marian thought that Timothy was just about the most disobedient piglet she'd ever known. She'd been in the barn the day he was born, and she remembered that he'd even given his mother a hard time, kicking and squealing the whole way out. He was still an ornery little pig, but she loved him just the same, from the end of his crinkled tail to the tip of his one black ear.

Just as she was about to finally corner Timothy, Marian spotted her friend Thomas the Woodsman coming down the road. His shoulders were bent beneath the weight of a huge ax.

"Thomas!" Marian greeted him with a smile. "How are you today?"

Thomas raised his head and gave Marian such a mournful look that there was no need for him to describe his feelings at that moment. Thinking that Thomas needed to be cheered up, Marian scooped the little pig into her arms and skipped across the yard, her long hair flapping behind her like a golden blanket in the wind.

"Where are you going?" she asked.

Thomas paused beside the gate and regarded Marian sadly with eyes as dark as the tangled beard that covered his face.

"Have you not heard the terrible news?" he asked. "The Sheriff's men are coming to collect yet another tax. If I don't give them half of my wood in payment, they'll take away my cottage and leave my family homeless. Not only that, they may throw me and my poor wife, Mary, into the dungeon. It has happened to others before me."

Marian shivered. The dungeon was an awful, rat-infested hole deep beneath the Sheriff's castle. No one tossed into it had ever emerged alive.

"But without that wood, how will you heat your home this winter?" asked Marian. "And what will you have to sell?"

"That I do not know," said Thomas. He shuffled his feet in the dust and drew in a deep breath. "Without a fire, my family and I could freeze. And without the money I'd make from selling the wood, we can't buy food and clothing. I don't know what's to become of us."

Marian furrowed her brow. Thomas worked on her

father's estate, but he and his wife, Mary, were more than just laborers to Marian. Ever since her mother, Lady Eleanor, had been lost in the woods two years earlier, Thomas and his wife had been practically like family.

"Ai-yeee!" The piglet in Marian's arms let out a sudden squeal. "Aiyee! Aiyee!"

Marian's blue eyes twinkled. "Timothy just said the Sheriff should mind his own business and quit taxing us to death."

Thomas returned Marian's smile. "You have a very wise pig there," he said. "How did you ever teach him to talk?"

Marian rubbed her knuckles along the pig's back and he squealed again. "Aiyee! Aiyee!"

"Getting him to talk isn't hard," she said. "All I have to do is rub him in the right spot. Of course, I can't understand what he's saying, but it's not too hard for me to make something up."

"You've a sharp wit for a girl of but thirteen," said Thomas. He gave Marian a pat on the shoulder. "You and your pig have made me smile for the first time all day." He paused for a moment and looked wistfully off into the distance. "If only your pig really could talk. Perhaps he'd be able to tell me how to save my wood."

"Perhaps he could," said Marian. She ran her tongue across her lips, narrowed her eyes, and put her clever mind into action. "Now, when exactly did you say the tax collectors were coming?"

"The day after tomorrow," said Thomas. "I'm sure they will stop here as well, especially considering the way your father often criticizes the Sheriff's cruel ways."

Marian looked back at the house. She could see her father staring out of an upstairs window. Since her mother had disappeared, her father's hair had gone gray, and he'd taken to wearing clothing as black as his judge's robes.

"No doubt the Sheriff will try to tax us doubly hard. He'd like nothing better than to drive my father and me from our estate and seize the land for himself," said Marian. She rubbed her chin and thought. Like water in a teakettle, a plan was beginning to bubble away in her head. "You know what? Maybe my piglet really can save us."

"This is no time for jokes," said Thomas. He wiped his nose with the back of a ragged sleeve. "In two days Mary and I could be in terrible trouble. Perhaps you and your father will be too."

"Not if Timothy has anything to say about it," said

Marian. She rubbed the pig's back and he let out a long, piercing squeal. "In fact, he just predicted the Sheriff's men will get neither your wood nor my father's gold."

Thomas eyed Marian as though she'd suddenly slipped her senses. "Please, Marian, I told you I'm in no mood for joking."

"The Sheriff's tax collectors may be strong, but they are not very smart," said Marian. "Trust me. I have a feeling everything will turn out fine."

Thomas shook his head, waved good-bye half-heartedly, and shuffled off down the road.

"Stop worrying!" called Marian after the departing woodsman. "Timothy will come to the rescue!"

Thomas raised a hand in farewell but didn't turn around. A few minutes later, bent beneath the weight of his giant ax, he crested a small hill and was gone.

Marian worked on her plan all the rest of the day. She wasn't sure whether it would work, but she knew she had to try, if only for the sake of her father. Ever since her mother had disappeared, she couldn't remember a single smile crossing his face. If the Sheriff succeeded in driving them from their estate, it would surely be the end of her father, and perhaps of all those who worked on his lands as well. She missed her mother too, and that is why she cared so much about defeating the Sheriff. When times had been difficult, her mother had always found a way to save them. Now Marian wanted to do the same.

The next morning she hurried to the estate of her best friend, a boy named Robert of Locksley, whom everyone called Robin. They had grown up together, and although Robin was a few years older than Marian, they had been friends for as long as either could remember.

"Robin!" she cried, pounding on the heavy wooden door. "I need your help!"

Many minutes later the door swung open and a tall, sandy-haired boy, thin as a wick, came outside, rubbing his eyes.

"Good heavens, Marian, do you know what hour it is?" he asked, shading his eyes against the brilliant sun. "I was sound asleep."

"We have no time to waste," said Marian. "I have a plan and I need your help."

Robin rolled his eyes skyward. "Please, not another one of your plans." He shook his head. "Your last scheme nearly cost us our lives. Remember when we snuck into the Sheriff's ball and filled our pockets with fruit for our hungry neighbors?"

"And we succeeded too," said Marian.

"Just barely," said Robin. "I was so weighed down with apples and pears that the Sheriff's soldiers nearly caught me running away."

Marian grinned, then looked around and lowered her voice. "We have to work fast. The tax collectors are coming tomorrow."

"I know," said Robin, nodding. "My father says that if we don't give the Sheriff half of our money, he may confiscate half of our estate."

"If my plan works, your father will have nothing to fear," said Marian. She put a hand on her friend's shoulder. "Can I count on you to help?"

"Help? What kind of help?" asked Robin cautiously.

"I just need you to spread the word about Timothy."

"Timothy? Who's he?"

"My talking pig," said Marian. "He predicts the future too. Sort of."

Robin laughed. "Is this a joke? Pigs don't talk."

Marian tapped her friend on the nose. "I'll explain everything later. Please. I can't do this all by myself."

When Robin hesitated, Marian raised two fingers

and held them out. "Two forever?"

Robin sighed. "All right, two forever," he said, touching Marian's fingers with the tips of his own.

Two forever. It was a ritual the pair had performed many times before. Two forever. That was the deal. When one asked for help, the other always had to agree, quickly and without complaint.

"Sooner or later your schemes are going to land us in the Sheriff's horrible dungeon," said Robin. "Tell me, my friend, is this going to be dangerous?"

"Of course it will be." Marian grinned. "If it weren't, it wouldn't be much fun, now would it?"

CHAPTER TWO

THE AMAZING, ASTOUNDING PIG

Tax collecting day dawned bright and sunny, but as the Sheriff's tax collectors, Simon and Norman, set out from town in their cart, dark clouds began sweeping in from the west, threatening rain.

At each house along the road, no matter how grand or how humble, they drew up to the door and called to the owners to come out.

"By the order of the Sheriff of Nottingham, bring out your taxes and place them in the cart!" cried Simon, who was wearing a tight leather cap ringed with silver spikes.

"Be quick about it or you'll find yourself in the castle dungeon and your home in ashes!" added Norman, who lacked both hair on his head and brains within.

"Here are some of my most valuable possessions," said Christopher the Hunter, carefully placing some of his finest arrows in the back of the cart. "However, I doubt that you will ever deliver them to the Sheriff. Timothy told me this will be a very unlucky day for you both."

"Timothy?" Norman whipped out his sword and touched it to Christopher's throat. "Who is this insolent fool?"

"Timothy isn't a fool. He's a pig. He predicts the future. And quite accurately too. Two days ago he told me that you would come precisely at this hour, and sure enough, here you are," he said, repeating to the tax collectors the very words Marian had instructed him to say.

"Nonsense," snorted Norman, withdrawing his sword. "Pigs don't talk." He raised a bushy eyebrow. "Unless, of course, he's a witch."

"Pigs can't be witches," said Simon. He snapped the reins and the cart lurched off down the road. "I've never heard such a ridiculous thing. Imagine, a pig that can predict the future."

At each house the story was the same.

"Here is my bag of rare spices," said Elizabeth the Innkeeper, placing the tan sack in the back of the cart. "And, Simon, I see you are wearing the leather hat Timothy predicted you would wear. I'm sure you'd agree he's a very amazing pig."

Simon took off his hat and examined it. "Really? He said I would wear this?"

"With silver studs circling the base," she said, describing the hat just as she saw it at that moment.

Simon shook his head. "Incredible."

"Indeed," said Elizabeth. "He's a wondrous animal."

At the next home Anne the Seamstress placed a fine velvet cloak with a fur trim in the back of the cart. She looked up at the darkening sky. Any fool could see that rain was coming. "Hurry up. I don't want this cloak to get wet before it can get to the Sheriff. Timothy predicted a storm."

Norman sniffed the air. "I think he's right again," he said. "A storm is coming. Do you think this amazing pig might be able to predict my own future?"

"Of course," said Anne, repeating the words Robin had told her to say. "Anyone can ask him anything. He's truly the most astounding pig in all of Sherwood Forest. Maybe the most amazing in the entire world!"

When the tax collectors stopped at the next home, Thomas the Woodsman quickly appeared, holding an armload of his precious wood. "You can come back for the rest later," he said, placing the wood in the back of the cart. "Timothy told me that this wood will never burn in the Sheriff's fireplace."

By now the tax collectors could no longer contain their curiosity.

"Tell us, Thomas, where can we find this astounding pig?" asked Simon.

"You'll find him at your next stop, the home of Maid Marian and her father, Geoffrey the Magistrate," said Thomas. He glanced up at the thick clouds. "Hurry now. It's going to pour."

And so, spurred on by the threat of rain and the promise that they'd soon meet Timothy the astounding pig, the tax collectors hurried to Marian's house.

When they arrived, they found Marian outside with a piglet in her arms, and her father, the judge, standing by her side, but they did not see Robin hiding behind a nearby tree.

"I have the Sheriff's tax money," said Geoffrey, showing Norman and Simon the coins inside a small leather bag. "I'll place it in the back of the cart."

"Do that and be quick about it," ordered Simon. "We must get back before the clouds burst."

"And they soon will," said Marian, for she had already felt a drop fall. "Timothy here has predicted a downpour."

"What? You're telling me that the piglet in your arms is the famous Timothy?" Norman sneered. "Why, that little runt couldn't predict the sunrise."

"Laugh if you wish," said Marian. "But Timothy is little only in size. His powers are grander than even those of the famous magician Merlin." She rubbed Timothy's back and the pig screeched, "Aiyeee!" "Did you hear that? He says he knows everything about your future."

"Really?" said Simon, leaning forward. Even Norman seemed suddenly interested. "All right then, tell us, little pig, will we find happiness and riches?"

"Perhaps," said Marian, approaching the cart. "Listen carefully to what Timothy has to say."

For the next few minutes Marian rubbed Timothy's back, and each time he squealed, she made up something about Simon's and Norman's futures.

"Oh my," said Marian. "He says you'll travel far and wide and be the guest in many fine castles."

"Is that so?" said Norman, smiling.

"Oh, oh," continued Marian, between the pig's squeals. "Looks like things won't always be so rosy. Bandits will try to rob you. They're going to steal all your money."

"What money?" asked Simon. "We're as poor as dung beetles."

Timothy squealed. "You may be poor now, but you'll soon find a great treasure," said Marian, telling them the first thing that popped into her head. "You two are going to very, very rich."

"I certainly like the way that sounds," said Simon.

All this time, while Simon and Norman were greedily following Marian's words and Timothy's squeals, Robin was removing the goods and gold from the back of the cart. As he took away each item, he substituted something else for it. Instead of the bags of coins, he placed sacks of rocks into the cart; instead of the arrows, he put sticks; instead of the wood, twigs; instead of the spices, manure; and in place of Anne's fine cloak, he put a rag. When he was done, Robin signaled to Marian and returned to his hiding place behind the tree.

"Timothy has one final prediction," said Marian.

She rubbed her pig's back and he squealed long and loud. "'Sadly,' he says, 'this will be an unlucky day for you both. In fact the Sheriff is going to be so displeased with the two of you that you'll both soon be out of a job.'"

"Nonsense," said Simon, shaking his head.

"Flumadiddle!" said Norman. "We are the best tax collectors the Sheriff's ever had."

Marian shrugged her shoulders. "I'm only reporting the pig's words," she said. "And he says the Sheriff will not be happy with the worthless things you have collected."

"Now I'm certain your pig doesn't know what he's talking about," said Simon. "Our cart is loaded with all the riches in the land."

Just then, before anyone, including Timothy the piglet, could say another word, the clouds split open and the rain began to pour down as though a dam had burst.

"Hurry!" cried Marian. "The road will soon be awash in mud."

"We're on our way!" called out Simon. He snapped the reins and the cart rattled away toward the Sheriff's castle.

Though it rained long and hard, Norman and Simon eventually arrived in Nottingham, a sad collection of huts and rough wooden houses clustered at the foot of the Sheriff's castle, a huge pile of stone and brick that loomed over the town like a giant, soot-blackened skull, casting a chill on everyone who fell beneath its awful shadow. After crossing a muddy moat, they passed through the gate and clattered into the castle courtyard, where the Sheriff was waiting to claim his precious taxes.

"It took you long enough to get here," he said, stroking a beard cut sharp as the letter V. He fixed his cold blue eyes on Norman. "The wait had better be worth it. What have you collected today?"

"See for yourself," said Norman, who, like Simon, was dripping like a wet rag. "The treasure is all in the cart."

The Sheriff stuck his head into the back of the cart. "What is this? Some kind of a joke?" He frowned, emptying rocks from the sacks and the leather bag. "Don't you know the difference between a stone and a nugget of gold?"

"But...but, sir," blubbered Simon. "I assure you we..."

"And what do you call this?" thundered the Sheriff,

holding up the rag.

"A cloak for you?" suggested Norman, wincing. "I certainly don't remember it looking like that when—"

"And here's something that stinks!" the Sheriff roared, opening the bag of manure. "What's this for?"

"Spice for your food?" whispered Simon.

"You dunderheads!" bellowed the Sheriff.

He pulled the sticks and twigs from the back of the cart and threw them to the ground. "You call this treasure? Do you take me for a fool!"

Simon and Norman looked at each other and gasped. "The things we collected *are* worthless," said Simon. "It's just as Timothy predicted!"

"Timothy?" asked the Sheriff. "Who is this Timothy? What are you two dolts talking about?"

"Timothy is a pig that predicts the future," explained Norman.

"Idiots!" thundered the Sheriff. "A pig can't predict the future!"

"But this is a special pig," Simon tried to explain. "There's not a creature in the land, man nor beast, that's as wise."

This did not make the Sheriff feel any better. "Are you saying a pig is smarter than I am?" he fumed.

Simon swallowed. "Well, he is pretty amazing, sir."

"That does it! You're fired, both of you!" shouted the Sheriff. He threw up his arms in exasperation. "I've never known such cabbage-headed morons."

All Norman and Simon could do was shake their heads in wonder. "Amazing," said Norman. "The pig predicted we'd lose our jobs. And we did. Marian and her pig are amazing!"

"Marian?" said the Sheriff. He narrowed his eyes. "That name sounds familiar."

"She's the daughter of Geoffrey the Magistrate," said Simon.

"Geoffrey!" roared the Sheriff. "I should have guessed that he was mixed up in this. That whole family's been nothing but trouble for the last five years." He stroked his beard. "Marian, huh. I'll make sure that little guttersnipe pays for this."

"If you want to blame anyone, blame the piglet," said Norman. "He did all the talking."

"Idiots! Piglets don't talk!" bellowed the Sheriff. He pointed a shaking finger at the castle gate. "Begone! Get out of my sight! Forever!"

Before the Sheriff could change his mind and throw them into the dungeon, Norman and Simon hopped off the cart and raced away into the countryside.

"And never come back!" yelled the Sheriff, shaking his fist at the fleeing men. Without thinking, he kicked at the worthless pile of goods at his feet. Bam! his toe rammed right into one of the stones.

"Ouch! Ow! Ow!" he roared, hopping up and down. "Blast it all! Marian is going to pay for this. Mark my words. By sundown tomorrow I'll see her clapped in chains and thrown into my dungeon!"

He grunted and rubbed his sore foot. Then, chuckling, he said, "And while she's down there in the dark, sharing a crust of bread with the rats, I plan to be feasting on a certain little talking piglet."

CHAPTER THREE

QUICKER THAN
A MOUSE

It was said in Sherwood Forest that the only thing quicker than Marian's wit was her hands. Her friend Robin liked to joke that Marian was so fast she could pick the fleas off a running dog, then slip the fleas into a miser's fist before either the dog or the man was the wiser.

What he didn't say was that those same hands could also catch mice better than any cat in the kingdom. As proof, she arrived in the dining room the next morning holding a little gray mouse by the scruff of the neck.

"Look what I found eating through our sack of grain," she said, dangling the creature in her father's face.

Her father, dressed as usual in black, looked up from his breakfast and forced a thin smile. "He has good taste. That was the most expensive grain at the market," he said. "Make sure you take him far from home before you release him."

"As you wish," said Marian, petting the mouse on the head with her finger. "Poor fellow was only trying to survive. Like all of us these days, I suppose."

Geoffrey sighed. His eyes grew moist. "I don't know what I'd do without you," he said. "Ever since your mother disappeared, you've been everything to me."

Marian leaned over and kissed her father's rough cheek.

"I worry about you," said Geoffrey. "You take too many chances. Like that mouse, someday you're going to get caught."

"I'm not like this guy," Marian said, staring into the frightened little face of the mouse. "I'm much too fast to catch."

"You have a will of your own, just like your mother. She, too, tried to protest the Sheriff's ways, and to this day I fear that awful man may have had something to do with her disappearance," said Geoffrey. He pushed himself away from the table. "You must be careful, my sweet Marian. You may be quicker than the Sheriff, but you're not stronger."

"Strength isn't everything," said Marian. She tapped her head. "Brains count for a lot. And we all know that even the village idiot has more smarts than our Sheriff."

Just then Marian heard voices and the clatter of boots in the hall.

KA-BAM!

Marian turned just as the door to the dining room was thrust open.

"An idiot am I?" bellowed the Sheriff himself, marching into the room in a pair of high leather boots, rough tan breeches, and a ruffled shirt. Three soldiers with drawn swords followed close behind.

Marian and her father froze in place, momentarily stunned.

"You insolent rapscallion!" roared the Sheriff, who had obviously been listening at the door. "You've taken me for a fool for the last time." He narrowed his dark eyes and stroked his sharp beard. "If you were any older, I'd have you hung."

Marian addressed the mouse still suspended between her fingers. "My, isn't he a kind fellow though?"

"You won't be mocking me after a few years in my dungeon," said the Sheriff. His face was as taut as a drum. "Do you realize that when you steal taxes from me, you're stealing from King Richard as well?"

Geoffrey leveled a finger at the Sheriff. "If Good King Richard knew how badly you treated his subjects, he'd have *you* thrown into the dungeon."

The Sheriff wheeled about and glared at the magistrate. "Watch your tongue, Geoffrey. Treason is a hanging offense."

Geoffrey snorted and turned away.

"Seize the girl," said the Sheriff. "And on your way out grab that talking piglet. I'd like to hear what he has to say when he learns he's on this evening's menu."

Geoffrey turned back, his face suddenly pale as parchment. "No, please. Don't take my daughter. She's only a girl."

"A few years in the dungeon will teach her some respect," said the Sheriff. He motioned to his men. "Go ahead. Take her away."

Before the soldiers could move, Geoffrey stepped between them and his daughter. "Wait! Perhaps we can make a deal."

The Sheriff lifted a single eyebrow. "Deal? What

kind of a deal?"

Geoffrey drew in a deep breath. "I've been saving a few gold coins. It's all the money I have."

"Go on," said the Sheriff.

"Would you grant Marian's freedom in exchange for the coins?"

The Sheriff stroked his beard. "That depends. How many are there?"

Geoffrey withdrew from the room and returned a few moments later, holding a cloth sack. "Is this enough?"

The Sheriff chewed on his lip and thought. Marian never doubted he'd decide in favor of the gold. If there was one thing she knew about the Sheriff, it was that he was guided in everything he did by one thing, and one thing alone: greed.

"Give me the sack," he said. "I want to make sure you haven't filled it full of rocks as you did before."

Marian looked down at the mouse still wiggling away between her fingers. The little fellow gave her an idea. If Timothy had helped save Thomas's wood, maybe the mouse could rescue her father's gold. Just maybe.

"Father, may I have the sack first?" she asked. "I think I left a coin of my own in there." She glared at the Sheriff. "It's one thing for my father to give away his gold, but I've made no such offer."

Marian's father gave her a curious look as he passed her the sack. Marian returned his look with a wink, then emptied the sack onto the table.

The sight of the gleaming coins, scores of them, caused the soldiers to gasp.

"I had no idea you had such riches," said the Sheriff, his eyes round as wagon wheels.

"There!" said Marian, pointing with her free hand. "That's my gold piece there."

"Leave it!" said the Sheriff, slapping the table so hard the coins jumped a foot. "Do you think I'd let you take away any of your ransom? Return every coin to the sack, and be quick about it!"

Marian grumbled to herself but did as she was told. When she was finished she gave the sack to the Sheriff.

"Thank you, Marian," said the Sheriff. He laughed. "Now who's the smart one, huh?"

"I was wrong," said Marian. She shrugged. "Maybe you are smarter than you look."

"A lot smarter than I look," said the Sheriff proudly. He motioned to one of the soldiers. "Tie that bag onto the back of my saddle. Then let's ride." He looked around. "The sooner we're out of this treasonous home the better."

"As you wish, sir," said the soldier.

The Sheriff touched a finger to his forehead. "Good day, Maid Marian. Be thankful your father's generosity has spared you from the dungeon—this time."

"Good day," said Marian, touching her own forehead. Then, as the Sheriff went out the door, she turned to her father and whispered. "Believe it or not, it is a very good day."

Geoffrey and Marian walked to the front door of the manor and watched the Sheriff and his men ride away.

"For a moment there I thought I'd lost you," said Geoffrey, hugging her close. He shook his head. "But what will we do now? That gold was nearly all the money we have."

"That money isn't going far," said Marian. "The mouse will make sure of that."

Geoffrey ruffled his brow. "The mouse? You mean the one you caught eating through our grain sack?"

"Just before I closed up the sack, I slipped him in with the gold," said Marian. "I'm sure by now he's already happily chewing his way out."

Geoffrey put a hand to his cheek. "So then that means..."

"That the gold will spill out on the road, coin by coin," said Marian. "All we've got to do is hurry down the road and pick it up. Won't the Sheriff be surprised when he finds the sack empty!"

Geoffrey's face darkened. He looked at his daughter with sudden horror. "Marian, good heavens, don't you see what you've just done?"

"Sure, I've tricked the Sheriff." She smiled. "What's wrong with that?"

"Everything," said Geoffrey. "If he thinks you are to blame, he'll be back here quicker than lightning, and just about as hot too."

Marian winced.

"I'll find the gold," said Geoffrey. He bent over until he was eye to eye with his daughter. "You must leave at once. Quickly, head for the Locksley estate before the Sheriff discovers what you've done."

"But if I leave, who will take care of you?" asked Marian.

Geoffrey's eyes suddenly flooded with tears. "Don't you understand, my sweet, sweet Marian? If you don't leave now, you'll be in the dungeon by nightfall."

"But, Father—"

"Just go," said Geoffrey, putting a finger to Marian's lips. "There's no telling how much time we have."

CHAPTER FOUR

THE FINEST ARCHER

Marian gave her father a final tearful hug. Then she hurried off into the woods and disappeared between the trees without looking back.

Marian could have found her way to Robin's house with her eyes closed. Though the path was rough and twisted, and crossed three streams, she never worried about getting lost. At night wolves could be heard howling from the darkness, calling the pack to the hunt, but during the day they were never a threat to man or beast.

Despite a few lingering storm clouds, the day turned out fine. Sherwood Forest was rich with the scent of pine. The air was full of bird songs, and the meadows were covered in the colors of springtime, newly ablaze with lilies and wild roses.

But Marian had little time to contemplate the wonders of nature. Her mind was filled with troubling matters. What if the Sheriff blamed her father for the loss of the gold? He'd said he couldn't hang Marian because of her age, but would he be so quick to spare the magistrate? Probably not. Ever since she'd left that morning, an awful truth had been gnawing at her brain: though she had not intended it, her simple trick had placed her father in mortal danger.

Fortunately, these awful thoughts were soon driven away by a sound she knew well.

Thunk! Thunk! Thunk!

"Robin!" she cried, bursting from the woods into a blaze of sunlight. "Hold your arrows!"

"My friend!" said Robin, lowering his bow. He'd been firing away at a small scrap of red cloth pinned to a distant bale of hay. Beyond the bale, across a wide field, stood Locksley Manor, Robin's home.

Even at his age Robin was considered one of the finest archers in Nottinghamshire. Marian didn't have to look to know that every one of his arrows had found its mark.

"The Sheriff wants to lock me in his dungeon," said Marian, jogging over to her friend.

Robin raised his bow and pointed it toward the woods. "The Sheriff? Is he chasing you this very minute?"

Marian put her hands on her knees and bent over to catch her breath. "No, but he will be soon enough," she said, looking up. Her face was red and beaded with sweat. "Can you hide me for a while?"

Robin raised two fingers. "Of course," he said.

Marian touched the fingers with her own. "Two forever."

Late that morning Robin's father, the Earl of Locksley, joined them for a meal served in the manor's grand hall. As they ate, Marian explained all that had happened that morning.

"I fear my father may be in as much danger as I am," she said.

"I fear you are right," said the Earl. His heavy cheeks sagged nearly to the fur-lined collar of his dull-green jacket. He paused to dip a crust of bread into his stew, then slowly shook his head. "The Sheriff is a powerful man. This time you may have pushed him too far."

"If only King Richard knew about the pain the Sheriff has inflicted on the poor people of Sherwood Forest," said Marian. "The king is famous for his kindness. If he knew the truth, surely he'd have the Sheriff removed."

"Perhaps, but the king is far away in London," the Earl said wearily. He glanced up at the heavy chandelier above the large oak dining table, then waved at the rich tapestries hanging on the manor walls. "Even a nobleman such as myself can't get a message through to the king. The only news he gets from the Forest comes by way of the Sheriff's messengers."

"But, Father, couldn't we send a message of our own?" asked Robin.

"The Sheriff's soldiers control the roads. Nothing and no one gets through without the Sheriff's approval."

Marian sighed. "I'm so worried about my father."

Robin's father reached out and patted Marian's hand. Marian spent so much time at the Locksley home that she was practically part of the family.

"Marian, I know your father. He'll be all right," said the Earl. "If you feel you must check on him, you can go at first light, no sooner."

"As you wish," said Marian. "It's just that—"

"It's just that you're in my care now," interrupted the Earl. "I must know where you're going and when you'll return."

"Very well then. We'll leave at first light and return by dark," Marian said. "I promise."

"Don't do anything foolish," said the Earl. "One girl cannot defeat the Sheriff and his soldiers. Not by herself." He paused and shook his head. "Look what happened to your mother. Some say she was taken by wolves while hunting. Others think the Sheriff's men may have killed her because she protested his harsh laws."

Marian looked down at her food. She'd barely touched her meal. Perhaps the Earl was right. One girl couldn't defeat the Sheriff. But that hadn't stopped her mother. She looked up.

And it wasn't going to stop her either.

CHAPTER FIVE

WOLVES

Just before dawn, with the slightest hint of red staining the horizon, Robin and Marian met at the bottom of the grand stairway in the front hall of Locksley Manor.

"Let's hurry," Marian said. "I've got to get to my father before the Sheriff does."

Without exchanging another word, they snuck out of the manor. Hurrying quietly across the moonlit field, they stole silently into the dark woods of Sherwood Forest.

"This isn't going to be easy," said Robin after they'd paused to catch their breath. In the distance the lone howl of a wolf broke the silence. Robin raised his bow. "I hope I don't have to use this along the way."

Marian looked up at the tall trees standing sentinel-like in the darkness. Then she turned to Robin, his face faintly lit by the pale moonlight. "I wish we could wait until the sun is all the way up, but every moment is precious. The Sheriff's men may be on their way back even now."

Robin nodded. "Then let's be on our way, my friend."

Neither Marian nor Robin had ever crossed the forest in the dark, but they knew the way by heart. In places the woods were so thick that they had to creep forward as though they were blind, their hands outstretched in front of them. In other places there was enough light to pick out the trail clearly. And in some spots the forest opened into meadows awash in light from the coming dawn, but they were careful to avoid these open spaces, for it was in such places where they were most likely to be taken by wolves.

The two rarely spoke during the journey. Their eyes were too busy straining to see, their ears too busy listening for danger, and their minds too focused on the tasks that lay ahead in their battle with the Sheriff and his men. Only the lonely calls of birds, the occasional rustling of the wind, and the crackling of the twigs beneath their feet broke the silence.

Marian spent much of the walk trying to think of a

way to get a message to King Richard. It was possible to elude the Sheriff's soldiers, but even if she got through to King Richard's castle, then what? Why would the king even agree to see her? She was just the daughter of one his many magistrates. No, a meeting seemed most unlikely.

SNAP!

Marian's thoughts stopped in midstream. Robin froze in his tracks. Something had stepped onto the path not ten feet away. It was too dark to make anything out, but there was something there. A glint of moonlight off an eye told them that much.

From behind them came the cry of a wolf, then another.

Marian swallowed. For a moment she thought she might faint. Her heart was beating so fast she was afraid it might pound right through her chest. Robin reached into his quiver, pulled out a single arrow, and fit it into his bow.

The wolves howled again, their cries rising in a horrible chorus.

"There must be five or more behind us," said Robin, searching the darkness.

"And some ahead of us," said Marian. She wished

she had a weapon. Bending down slowly, she picked up a long stick. If she were going to die, she at least wanted to go down fighting.

Suddenly something came crashing through the brush at the edge of the trail. Without thinking, Robin shot an arrow. He heard a yelp and knew he'd made a hit. But now, before he could fix another arrow into his bow, the woods came alive with wolves. They seemed to be everywhere at once, howling, snarling, crashing through the brush, their dark figures flashing in and out of the moonlight.

Marian's first thought was to run. But where? She knew the way ahead was blocked. To the rear and the sides were the onrushing wolves. She braced for an attack, raising the arm holding the stick in front of her and putting her other arm up to protect her throat.

Robin fumbled for another arrow. "There are too many!" he shouted. "They're everywhere!"

Then all at once there was a tremendous commotion just ahead on the trail. The wolves' cries rose to a scream. Something was on the ground. Suddenly there was dust in the air along with the groans of a dying animal.

"They've got a deer!" whispered Marian. "That's what was on the road ahead of us."

"No wonder they passed us by. They were after bigger game," said Robin.

In the moonlight Marian could see his thin face was beaded with sweat. Her face was too. "Quickly," she said, taking Robin by the elbow. "Once the wolves are finished with the deer, we'll be next."

The pair waited a moment to make sure the way was clear. Then they dropped off the path and skirted around the feasting wolves.

Marian shuddered as they passed close by the fallen deer. "That could have been us," she said.

"That deer saved us," said Robin. "We owe him our lives."

Marian knew it was true, and she spoke a silent prayer of thanks to the fallen animal.

They half-walked, half-sprinted the rest of the way, finally emerging from the woods at the edge of the road. Marian's home stood before them in the moonlight, silent and dark.

Quietly, on cats' feet, they slowly approached the house.

"Everything looks all right from here," whispered Robin.

And from the outside it did.

But that was only from the outside.

CHAPTER SIX

THE REWARD

"Oh no!" exclaimed Marian when the door that should have been locked swung open. "Father!"

"What's wrong?" asked Robin, peering over her shoulder.

"Father!" she cried again, squinting into the darkness.

"Anyone home?" called Robin.

"Father!" cried Marian, stepping boldly into the main hall. "Answer me! Are you here?"

When no one replied, Marian quickly located a candle and carried it to the hearth in the sitting room, where a few coals still remained from the last fire. After touching the wick to an ember, she blew softly and coaxed the candle to life. As the flickering flame illuminated the large room, she gasped.

"Oh...great heavens!"

The place looked as though it had been visited by a whirlwind. The furniture had been overturned; the stuffing had been yanked from the chairs and sofas; and vases, statues, and pillows had been scattered about the floor.

Marian lifted the candle high above her golden hair and scanned the room. "Well, at least there wasn't much of a fight."

"Are you blind?" said Robin. "Look at this place. How can you say there wasn't a fight?"

"Because there's not a drop of blood anywhere. No, this wasn't a battle. It was a search."

"For what?"

"For what I hope is still in my father's special hiding place," said Marian, reaching up into the chimney above the hearth. She fumbled around for a moment, then drew out a heavy sack.

"Here's the gold my father must have picked up on the road yesterday." She glanced down at the sack and sighed. "It's just as my father guessed. The Sheriff came riding back as soon as he realized he'd been tricked." She touched a finger to the hearth. "I'd say they probably arrived around sunset, judging by the warmth still in the stones."

Robin peered uneasily about the jumbled room. Something terrible had happened there, and a sense of evil still hung in the air like a wisp of acrid smoke.

"Maybe your father escaped," he suggested hopefully.

Marian put the sack back into its hiding place and walked back out into the main hall, holding the candle in front of her. "Unlikely," she said. "His bow is hanging on the wall out here. My father wouldn't have left it behind."

"Then he was taken away?"

"Aye! That he was!" came a voice from the front door.

Marian jumped a foot. Robin too. Unseen, Thomas the Woodsman had entered the house while they were talking.

Marian put a hand over her heart. "Thomas! I very nearly leapt out of my shoes," she said. She paused a moment to calm her heart, then continued. "What about my father? What did you see?"

"I wish I didn't have to bring you such sad news," said Thomas. "But it's just as you feared. The Sheriff came back late in the day complaining that his gold had spilled onto the road. He said they had searched the road, but hadn't found as much as a penny. When he demanded another sack of gold, your father refused and he was arrested. After he was taken away, a few of the men stayed behind to search for the gold." He gestured at the ruined room. "That's when they did this."

"It's all my fault," said Marian. "I thought I was so clever when I hid that mouse in the sack." She lowered her head and brushed away a tear. "I should have known he would come back for my father. I should have known it!"

Thomas placed a worn hand on Marian's shoulder. "Don't blame yourself," he said. "This day was going to come soon enough. The Sheriff hates your father and covets his lands." He raised Marian's chin with his finger. "He's an evil man who destroys anyone who gets in his way. Your family, unfortunately, has been in the way for a long time."

"Your father hasn't broken any laws," said Robin. "Surely the Sheriff can't hold him for long, can he?"

"That's not the proper question," said Marian. She sniffled back her tears, then drew herself up to her full height and set her jaw. "The real question, my friends, is how long will it take us to break him out?"

Thomas gasped. "Break him out? But he's probably in the castle dungeon. No one has ever escaped from that awful place. Not ever."

"If we can't break him out, then I'll just have to think of something else," said Marian. There was a sense of determination in her voice that was as hard as iron. "One way or another I plan to see my father freed."

Robin groaned. "Marian, you're going to be the death of me yet."

"Robin," called Marian as she suddenly made her way for the open door, "I just remembered something else the Sheriff threatened—he said he was going to grab Timothy and have him for a meal. Oh, he probably sent his men to the barn as well!"

Marian rushed to the outbuildings in the back of the manor, finding her way in the pale light of the new sun. She pushed the barn door open and headed straight back to a fenced-in area where a large sow and her piglets were sleeping in the hay. As she came near, she heard a familiar squeal. "Aiyee!"

"Timothy!" cried Marian. She reached through the fence and patted him on the head in the darkness. "If only you really could tell me what the future will bring, I'd know best how to go about saving my father. As it is, I'm going to have to rely on my own wits."

The piglet quietly squealed as Marian stroked his back. Then Marian scooped him up in her arms and carried him back to the house, where Robin and Thomas stood talking. Thomas agreed to take Timothy back to his place. He didn't have much of a barn, but he promised that Timothy would be safe.

As it turned out, Marian had returned from the barn not only with a piglet but with a plan as well. So as soon as Thomas left, she got busy with needle and thread, preparing two disguises, and with quill and ink, preparing a letter to King Richard. It was a rare woman in those days who could read and write, and an even rarer girl. Marian had learned her letters from her mother and she was proud of her abilities, but it was a skill she had to hide. The Sheriff didn't like people who could read. He considered them a danger. The ability to read and write always conveyed power, and that was one thing the Sheriff did not want the people of Nottingham to have.

"The king must know the truth about the Sheriff," Marian told Robin, showing him the letter. "I've told him all about how we have been taxed to death, and that anyone who objects, including the magistrate, is cast into the dungeon."

Robin read the parchment. "It's a good letter," he told her.

Marian blew the ink dry, then signed her name. Robin signed his name beneath Marian's.

Marian carefully folded the parchment into a perfect square. Then she opened her vest and showed Robin the square of cloth she had stitched to the inside to make a hidden pocket. "There," she said, tucking the letter into the pocket. "Now all I have to do is find a way to get my letter into the king's hands."

"That's not going to be easy," said Robin.

"I didn't say that it would be," said Marian. "Nothing worth doing is ever easy, but that doesn't mean it can't be done."

Robin and Marian spent the rest of the morning cleaning up the house— putting furniture back in its place and sweeping away broken odds and ends. The house had not felt so empty since the night her mother had disappeared.

After resting for a bit and eating a late breakfast of cold potatoes and hard bread, Robin and Marian set out for Nottingham disguised as Gypsies.

"Are you sure we won't be found out?" asked Robin. He was wearing gray pants and a colorful jacket patched together by Marian from bits of cloth she'd found at the house. Marian had made herself a long patchwork skirt with a big pocket in the front. To complete her costume, she'd added copper bracelets to her wrists and a blue bandanna to her hair. A purple veil hid her face.

Robin had darkened his face with ashes and done the same to his hair, but even so, he didn't think he looked at all like an old Gypsy.

"Don't worry, you look fine," said Marian. "When we get to the castle, just remember to stoop over so that no one can see your face."

Robin nodded. "So what do we do when we get to the castle?"

"Nothing. Not today," said Marian. "Since it's a market day in Nottingham, we'll just blend in with the crowd and see what we can learn about my father. Then, once we know exactly where he is and how he's being guarded, we can work out a plan to free him."

Robin kicked at a clod of dirt on the road and sent it flying into the bushes. "I wish I could have brought my bow. What if we get into a fight?"

"The Sheriff doesn't allow weapons to be brought into town," said Marian. "You know that. But don't worry. When we come back we'll be armed. I can promise you that."

It took them nearly two hours to reach Nottingham. As it was market day, and warm and sunny besides, the dusty town square was alive with townsfolk and peasants exchanging goods and food. The smell of a chicken roasting on a spit mixed in the air with the laughter of children, the squealing of pigs, and the sweet sounds of a flute played by a strolling musician. There was so much to see and do that no one paid any more attention to the two Gypsies than they did to the man juggling fat onions, the acrobats walking on their hands, or the merchant selling roots he said would restore a bald man's hair.

Marian took a penny from the huge pocket in the front of her skirt and offered to buy two meat pies from a lumpy-faced man in a three-cornered hat.

"Tell me, kind sir. What's the news of the day?" she asked, placing the penny onto the man's huge, grime-caked palm.

"Why don't you tell me?" he said, seizing Marian by the wrist. He chuckled and leaned in so close she could make out the tangle of veins in his thick nose. "Why should I be telling you the news? You're the fortune teller."

Marian swallowed hard and tried to pull back, but

the man tightened his grip and pulled her closer still.

"Perchance the little Gypsy will read my future," he said in a low, gravely voice. His breath was thick as fog and reeked of stale garlic.

Marian looked over at Robin from behind her veil, then pulled back far enough to quickly survey the man.

"I…umm…see money in your future," she stuttered, playing the fortune teller. She was thinking that she was getting pretty good at this fortune-telling business—first her partnership with Timothy the pig, and now this.

"Money? In my future?" asked the man.

"Enough money to keep you in blackberry pies for the rest of your life," said Marian confidently. "Those pies are your favorites, aren't they?"

The man let go of Marian's hand and eyed her with astonishment. "How did you know I like blackberry pies?"

Marian never ceased to be amazed at people's gullibility. The man's love of berry pies was written all over him, literally. The front of his jacket was stained with their remains. Not only did she know what kind of food he liked, but she also could have told him he was a sloppy eater.

Marian scooped up the two meat pies and handed one of them to Robin. "Come. Let's go."

"Wait!" shouted the man, clawing at the air. "Tell me more. Just when will I make my fortune? And how?"

Marian never looked back. Within moments they'd left him far behind and disappeared into the swirling crowd.

"That man was an even bigger fool than the Sheriff's tax collectors," said Marian. She took a bite of the meat pie, then licked her lips. "I will say this though, he's a good cook."

Robin sniffed the pie, then took a bite. "Very tasty. Perhaps we should buy some more."

"I'd have to be starving before I got within that man's reach again," said Marian.

Suddenly the air was split by the sounds of a trumpet, followed closely by the shouts of the town crier, who was standing high on the stone steps leading to the castle.

"Hear ye! Hear ye!" he bellowed. "All hail the Sheriff of Nottingham bringing us glorious news!"

There was another blast from the trumpeter, and the Sheriff himself, followed by a company of his soldiers, descended from the castle. Everything stopped in the square. Few people believed he was truly bringing glorious news. More likely he was about to announce another round of taxes or claim more of the forest for himself.

Marian noted a line of soldiers lining the castle parapets and another group clustered near the huge front door. Getting inside the castle and down into the dungeon would not be easy, maybe even impossible. If she hoped to free her father she was going to need either a great plan or a lot of help. Most likely she would need both.

"There are traitors free in our land!" shouted the Sheriff, raising his arm. "People who would bring me down, and King Richard as well."

He stroked his black beard and surveyed his subjects. "Last night we captured one of the knaves, Geoffrey the Magistrate. Now I'm asking you to help me find the others, especially the magistrate's daughter, Maid Marian."

Marian bit her lip. She didn't mind fame, but not this kind!

The people in the square had little love for the Sheriff. He had treated them harshly and cruelly for years. If he needed help, he'd have to look elsewhere.

The Sheriff reached into his jacket pocket and

plucked out a fat gold coin. "Did I mention the reward?" he said. "Bring me the girl and this will be yours."

A murmur passed through the crowd. A gold coin was nothing to dismiss lightly.

Robin looked about uneasily. Would his neighbors really turn in Marian in exchange for a piece of gold? Probably not. But it was obvious from the talk going on around him that at least a few were considering it.

"Marian," whispered Robin, poking her in the side, "let's go before someone recognizes us."

"Not until I get that coin," said Marian.

"What? Are you crazy?" said Robin, trying to hide his face behind his hand. "Do you plan to turn yourself in for the reward?"

"For all I know, that coin could have been stolen from my father," said Marian. "If so, it's not the Sheriff's to give away. I intend to retrieve it."

Robin was too stunned to speak. In the meantime, the Sheriff had returned the coin to his pocket and descended the stairs.

"Make way for the Sheriff!" shouted one of his soldiers, parting the crowd. "Move aside, peasants!"

Robin turned away as the Sheriff approached, but not Marian.

"Sheriff!" she called from behind her veil. "I believe I can help you find that traitor!"

The Sheriff halted and looked around. "Who spoke?"

"Over here," said Marian, weaving her way through the crowd. "It is I, Sofia, who offers to help."

The Sheriff eyed Marian suspiciously. "And how can a young Gypsy girl help me?"

Marian touched her forehead, then drew in close to the Sheriff and whispered up into his long, bearded face. "There is much I know. Did your tax collectors not bring you sticks and stones the other day instead of goods and gold?"

The Sheriff nodded. "Yes, how did you know?"

"Listen to her. She knows everything," said the lumpy-faced meat-pie man, suddenly appearing from the crowd. "She knew all about me." He grinned. "Said I'd soon come into a fortune."

The Sheriff raised an eyebrow. "You? A fortune? Why, the rats in my cellar will sooner be turned into lords and ladies!"

"I swear," said the man, raising his hand. "She has the gift."

The Sheriff snorted, then rolled his eyes. "All right then. Tell me," he said wearily. "Where will I find that little gutter rat?"

Marian nodded. "She's closer than you think," she said. "My senses tell me she's hiding in this very village at this very moment."

The Sheriff considered Marian's words and stroked his goatee. "You wouldn't be trying to flumadiddle me, would you?"

"No, sir," said Marian, touching his arm. "Like you, I only wish to see that little traitor in prison."

The Sheriff gave Marian a thin smile. "All right then. My soldiers will search the town. We'll see if you truly do have the gift."

"She's under your very nose," said Marian, raising her hand. "I swear it."

"Then my men will find her quickly enough," said the Sheriff.

Marian held out her hand. "I believe you owe me a reward, sir. You offered a gold coin."

"You've told me nothing," scoffed the Sheriff. He waved at Marian with the back of his hand. "Scat! Begone, you witch."

"Wait, you promised!" said Marian, grabbing the Sheriff by the jacket. "Give me the reward."

"Begone, I said!" He snarled and brushed away her

hand. "Get away before I have you clapped in irons."

Marian glared up at the Sheriff. "You'll be sorry. A curse on you, sir!"

"Bah!" said the Sheriff, walking away. "You're a plague on the town. Begone!"

Marian turned and grabbed Robin. "Let's go!" she whispered.

Robin didn't have to be told twice it was time to leave. "That was a waste of time," he said as they sprinted away through the crowd. "I could have told you he wouldn't give you that coin."

Just then a voice rose above the clamor in the square.

"I've been robbed! My gold coin!"

"Marian!" gasped Robin, coming to a halt.

Marian grinned and opened her hand. The coin glowed back at Robin like the noonday sun. "I picked it from his pocket when I grabbed his jacket."

"You're amazing," said Robin.

Apparently the Sheriff thought she was pretty special too.

"Find that Gypsy girl!" he shouted. "Two gold coins to the one who brings me that thief, dead or alive!"

CHAPTER SEVEN

THE UNEXPLORED FOREST

Robin and Marian shot off like scared rabbits. Without so much as a backward glance, they ran through the village gates and sprinted for the forest. When they reached the safety of the trees, they paused to catch their breath and remove some of their bright Gypsy clothes.

"I've got an idea," said Robin. He took Marian's bandanna and veil, placed them atop his jacket, then crouched low and ran along the tree line until he was a considerable distance away. Then he draped everything over a bush and quickly returned to Marian's side.

"What are you trying to do? Throw the Sheriff off our trail?" asked Marian.

"It shouldn't be that hard," said Robin. He smiled. "The man is such a dunce."

Marian returned his smile, then pointed back at the village gate. "Look. Here comes that dunce now."

It was the Sheriff himself. He'd just come riding through the gate at the head of a company of his soldiers, their armor gleaming in the sun.

The Sheriff raised his sword and called his soldiers to a halt. For a while everyone milled about, gesturing toward the spot where Robin had placed the clothes.

"Maybe they're not going to come after us," said Robin.

"Don't count on it," said Marian. "I know that greedy Sheriff. He won't give up the chase until that gold is back in his pocket."

Sure enough, a few minutes later the Sheriff waved his sword and started toward the woods. The others followed at a slow gallop, their horses' hooves lifting high to avoid the rocks scattered across the field.

"Time to be on our way," said Marian, turning into the forest. "Your decoy has probably bought us some time, but we may need every moment of it if we hope to stay alive."

Robin looked back at the Sheriff, then followed her quickly into the woods. Without exchanging a word, they cut through a little meadow, jumped a stream, and picked up a deer trail that headed south into a part of the forest neither of them had ever explored.

At first they made good time on the well-worn path, but soon the trail dwindled down to nothing and they found themselves cutting through the raw forest, leaping fallen logs and dodging amongst the trees. From time to time they paused to catch their breath, but they never rested long. They couldn't afford to. Just as they started to relax, they heard shouts and the sounds of horses crashing through the brush, and they knew the Sheriff had picked up their trail once again.

"I swear, that man is harder to shake than a burr," said Marian.

Late in the afternoon they arrived at a little stream surrounded by giant oaks. It was the first water they'd seen in hours, and without hesitation, they threw themselves on their stomachs and drank deeply from the shallow brook.

"That Sheriff means to run us down like dogs," said Robin, raising up his head. "How much longer do you think we can keep going?"

In the distance Marian could hear the Sheriff and his men exchanging shouts and encouragement.

"They went that way!" came a faint voice.

"We've got them now," cried someone else.

"Dead or alive," said the Sheriff.

Marian already felt half dead. Her legs ached, and so did her stomach. They hadn't eaten anything since the meat pies earlier that morning.

Worst of all, Marian had no idea where they were. They'd twisted and turned so many times they could be almost anywhere. It was bad enough to be pursued by the Sheriff, but if night caught them in the forest, they'd also be dodging the wolves.

Marian pointed across a little clearing. "Climb up that big oak over there. See if you can get high enough to figure out where we are."

Robin pulled himself up on his elbows. His cheeks had been slashed in a dozen places by branches and brush. One of his pant legs had been ripped nearly in two, down below his knee.

"You go up," he said wearily, his eyes half closed. "You got us into this mess."

Marian was too tired to argue. She picked herself up and cocked an ear. Nothing. Only the sounds of the brook broke the silence. "Good," she thought, hoping that the Sheriff had lost their trail.

She found a low branch on a tall, twisted oak and boosted herself into the tree. After pausing for a moment to survey the best route, she began scrambling up the branches, nimble as a squirrel. She was halfway to the top when she suddenly heard someone coming up below her. It was Robin.

"What are you...?"

Robin put a finger to his lips and stopped her in midsentence.

Marian wrinkled her brow. Robin nodded toward the edge of the clearing where a soldier astride a horse silently surveyed the scene.

Marian stifled a gasp with her fist. Robin hunched below a thin branch and held his breath.

"They came this way!" cried the soldier, turning back. "Over here."

"Do you see anyone?" It was the Sheriff's voice.

"No, sir," shouted the soldier, cupping his hand alongside his mouth. "I see only tracks."

While the soldier's attention was diverted, Robin scampered up to where Marian sat straddling a huge branch.

"That was close," he whispered.

"Shhh," said Marian. She placed a finger to his lips

just as the Sheriff and his men came riding into the clearing. "We're not out of this yet."

The Sheriff halted his horse, then lifted his nose and sniffed at the air as though searching for the pick-pocket's scent. "They're close, my friends. Very close."

"They must have rested here," said a fat, red-faced soldier, dismounting from his horse. "I spotted fresh footprints by the stream."

The Sheriff cast his eyes about the clearing. Once he even glanced up into the trees, but somehow he missed Robin and Marian. He stroked his goatee and sniffed the air again. "Something rotten is riding the wind, all right. And no doubt it's that Gypsy thief and her friend."

One by one, the men in the clearing climbed down from their horses and made their way to the stream. Everyone drank, horses included.

"They probably took to the water," said the Sheriff after drinking deeply from his cupped hand. He wiped his mouth with the back of his sleeve, then rose to his feet. "My guess is that they're heading downstream. They'll use the water to hide their tracks." The Sheriff smiled. "They'll have to step ashore sometime though, and we'll pick up their trail then."

"Begging your pardon, sir, but isn't it getting a little late?" asked one of the soldiers, a fat-nosed man in dirty black boots. "It's soon going to be dark."

The Sheriff eyed the man curiously. "So?"

"The wolves, sir."

"The wolves are of no concern to me," said the Sheriff sharply. "I care only about catching that girl who stole my coin. The very insolence! The disrespect!" He snorted, dismissing the man with the back of his hand. "Prepare some soup. We'll eat and then move on."

Marian rolled her eyes. Robin groaned. Like it or not, they were about to become guests at the Sheriff's next meal.

CHAPTER EIGHT

THE SOUP

The soldiers soon had a fire going just a few steps from the very oak in which Marian and Robin were hiding. Then one of the men took a large iron pot out of a sack and filled it with water. The cook, who turned out to be the fat-nosed man, added a few potatoes and a bit of gray meat to the water. Then he placed the pot atop the fire and waited for it to boil.

Robin sniffed the vapors rising from below and made a face. "The Sheriff was right," he whispered. "There is something rotten in the wind, but it's probably only his supper."

"The smell isn't coming from below," Marian whispered back. "It's coming from this tree."

"Huh?" said Robin. He dropped his nose and smelled his armpit. "You blaming me?"

Marian rolled her eyes. She looked down at the soldiers milling about the clearing, then pointed to a bird's nest on a nearby branch. "That's where the stink is coming from. There are some abandoned eggs in there. I'm pretty sure they've gone bad."

Robin leaned toward the nest and sniffed. "EEE-yew, you're right," he whispered, making a face. "Looks like we hid in the wrong tree."

Marian smiled. "Maybe not," she said. "I've been thinking."

Robin winced. "I don't like it when you think," he said.

Marian smiled in reply, then put a finger to her lips and returned her attention to the Sheriff's men.

Some of them were resting in the clearing, three were tending to the fire, and a few others were sitting by the stream talking quietly among themselves.

Just about everyone was relaxing in one way or another, except the Sheriff. He spent most of his time pacing nervously about the clearing, occasionally pausing long enough to glance up at the dimming sky or to berate the cook for not getting the soup to boil faster.

At one point he went over to his horse, fumbled around for a minute in his saddlebags, then called out to one of the men sitting by the stream. "Bertram! Step over here. Be lively now!"

Bertram, who was almost as tall as a tree, hefted himself up and lumbered over to where the Sheriff continued to search through the saddlebag.

"Sir, how may I be of service?" asked Bertram, bowing.

"Blast it all!" yelled the Sheriff, suddenly dumping the contents of the bag onto the ground. "Where is that confounded letter?"

Bertram stepped back, startled by the Sheriff's sudden outburst.

"I remember placing it in the bag myself," said the Sheriff sharply. He looked around at his soldiers, then dropped his voice. "The land is crawling with thieves these days. You can't trust anyone."

Bertram bent over and picked up a handful of papers, as well as a black, leather-bound portfolio bulging with paper. "Could it be one of these, sir?"

"No, of course not, you fool," said the Sheriff without even looking.

"Perhaps it got stuck inside this portfolio," said Bertram, fanning through the sheaf of papers within. "That can happen sometimes. Once, in fact—"

WHAM! The Sheriff snatched away the portfolio in midsentence. "Don't you ever, ever look through my things!" he ordered. Marian had never seen the Sheriff so angry. His face was all twisted up and as red as a hot coal. "What did you see in there?"

Bertram swallowed and hunched up his shoulders. "I...I didn't see anything," he stammered. "I can't even read, sir."

The Sheriff growled, then drew his sword and pointed it at Bertram's throat. "Swear you didn't see anything!"

"I...I...I swear," Bertram said, raising his hands. Everyone else in the clearing turned to see what would happen next. For a moment, everything was still. The Sheriff had a terrible temper. It wouldn't have surprised a soul if he suddenly decided to carve a slice out of Bertram's Adam's apple.

Up in the tree, Marian was on the move. She knew that as long as the Sheriff's sword was drawn, no one would be looking up. Quick as a chipmunk, she skittered out to the nearby abandoned bird's nest.

"Marian! What are you doing?" Robin silently mouthed the words.

Wasting no time, Marian gingerly picked up each

of the rotten eggs and one by one dropped them like stones, plop! plop! plop!, into the boiling pot of soup. Not a soul, not even the cook himself, saw Marian add the new ingredients to the pot.

Robin put a hand over his mouth to stifle a giggle. Marian turned and winked, then scampered back to Robin's side. The whole operation had taken less than a minute.

After what must have seemed like hours to Bertram, the Sheriff finally put away his sword. "Hummpf," he snorted. "From now on, keep your hands off my private things. Is that clear?"

"Ya…ya…Yes, sir," said Bertram, his legs shaking as much as his voice.

The Sheriff looked about at his men. "What are you all staring at?" he barked sharply.

The soldiers quickly turned away.

The Sheriff snorted. Then, just as he was returning the portfolio to the bag, he noticed something at the bottom of the pouch.

"Ah, here's what I wanted, stuck in the lining it was," he said, fishing out a piece of folded parchment. "I want you to carry this to King Richard."

"I'm at your service, my lord," said Bertram, bowing. "Have I ever disappointed you in the past?"

"And I know you won't fail me this time," said the Sheriff. He pulled a quill and a small bottle of ink from a pouch on the side of his saddlebag, dipped the quill into the ink, and then scrawled his signature at the bottom of the letter. "This letter requests money from the king to help me defend his lands." He gave Bertram's shoulder a hard squeeze. "I need that money, my friend. Make sure you place the letter directly into the king's hands."

"I'll...I'll do exactly as you say," said Bertram. His voice still quivering. "You can be sure of that."

"The king's land doesn't need defending," whispered Marian. "I bet all that money will be going directly into the Sheriff's fat pocket."

"Be back in time for the festival in four days," said the Sheriff, again placing his hand on Bertram's shoulder. He smiled thinly. "The main attraction will be a special hanging. These tax protesters are going to be taught a lesson."

Marian gulped. "Hangings?" she thought.

"Supper!" cried the cook, banging on the pot. "Come. Let's eat."

Bertram walked the Sheriff's letter over to his own

horse and placed it in his leather saddlebag. Then he joined the rest of the company at the fire.

"Eat hearty, men," said the cook as he ladled out the soup into cups. "I think you'll agree I've outdone myself once again."

"Bah!" said the Sheriff, lifting his cup to his lips. "Outdoing yourself wouldn't take much. That last batch of broth you brewed tasted like rat innards!"

The soldiers laughed and raised their own cups in a mock toast to the chef.

"Drink it down quickly," commanded the Sheriff. "We can't let that Gypsy woman get too far ahead."

As one, the soldiers threw back their heads and downed their soup in a few gulps.

When their heads came back up, there was a moment of stone silence. The Sheriff's face twisted up to one side, then to the other. All the color left his cheeks. Tears flooded his eyes.

Marian grinned.

"Eeee-yew!" bellowed the Sheriff, just as the rotten eggs reached his stomach.

"Eee-yuck!" cried Bertram.

"We've been poisoned!" yelled someone else.

Some people threw back their heads and groaned.

Others grabbed their stomachs. The cook himself bent over and tried to spit out his own meal.

For a moment, everyone ran around in circles, certain they were about to croak. Then someone yelled, "Water!" and they stampeded toward the stream like cattle.

Marian put a hand over her mouth and giggled. Robin laughed out loud, but no one heard him. The Sheriff and his soldiers didn't care about anything at that point except washing away the taste of the rotten-egg soup. Lined up like hogs at a trough, they looked as though they were trying to drink the stream dry.

"Shall we be on our way?" asked Marian cheerfully.

Robin returned her smile and waved his hand with a royal flourish. "After you, my lady."

With one eye on the soldiers and the other on the next limb, the two quickly scooted down the tree.

When Marian reached the ground, she reached into her secret pocket and removed the letter she'd written to King Richard earlier that morning. "Why don't we let Bertram deliver this for us," she said.

"A splendid idea," said Robin, dropping to the ground.

Marian sprinted over to where Bertram's horse stood silently, his head bowed. She hurriedly opened the saddlebag and took out the Sheriff's letter, replacing it with her own.

Robin shot a look at the soldiers beside the stream. Their bellows and moans were growing less frequent. "We'd better get out of here," he said.

But Marian wasn't quite ready to leave. There was one more thing she needed, the little black portfolio the Sheriff had snatched back from Bertram.

Quickly, she ran over to the Sheriff's horse and plucked it from his saddlebag.

"Marian! Hurry!" whispered Robin, glancing over at the soldiers.

Marian waved the portfolio in reply.

"Let's go!" he whispered with renewed urgency.

Marian opened the portfolio and began to skim through the sheaf of parchment papers.

After a moment she looked up. "Robin! This portfolio is full of records! It's proof that the Sheriff has been stealing from the king."

Robin looked at the Sheriff and his soldiers still stretched out by the stream. "Marian. You can explain everything later. Let's go!"

Marian shot a look at the soldiers, then reached into the pouch on the Sheriff's saddlebag and took out his quill and ink. A few moments later she was back at Bertram's horse, adding a few words to her letter to the king. Hastily, she wrote that she'd found actual proof of the Sheriff's misdeeds in the tax records penned by the Sheriff's own hand—records that showed that the Sheriff spent the king's money on fine clothes and fancy jewels. At the bottom of the letter, Marian pleaded for the king to come to Nottingham before the Sheriff could carry out the hangings at the festival in four days' time. "The lives of your loyal subjects are at stake," she added. "And very possibly," she thought, "my own father's."

"Marian!" said Robin.

Marian looked up.

Some of the soldiers had stopped drinking and were getting to their feet. Luckily, she hadn't yet been spotted.

"Men, mount up!" called the Sheriff.

Marian returned the letter to Bertram's saddlebag. She then ducked down behind the Sheriff's horse, replaced the quill and ink, and skittered away to join Robin just beyond the clearing. Once she was out of sight, Marian dug a hole in the mulch and the leaves, took out the parchment records from the leather portfolio, and buried the portfolio. Then she slipped the records into her secret pocket.

They paused to make sure they hadn't been seen, then picked up a trail and followed it into the woods.

"I bet those guys won't soon forget that soup," said Robin as they picked their way through the brush.

"They won't have any choice," said Marian. "For the next month they're going to be tasting those rotten eggs every time they burp."

CHAPTER NINE

NIGHT

Marian and Robin couldn't afford to spend much time congratulating themselves on their latest escape. They may have been momentarily free of the Sheriff, but already the sun was setting and the world about them was quickly dimming. With night would come the cold—and the wolves. Nothing around them looked familiar. Anything could be behind the next tree, around the bend, or over the next rise.

They ran on for another hour in the growing darkness, searching for the road home. But in the end they were no closer to escape. In the distance an owl's hoot was answered by another. Then a wolf started up, and before long, a chorus of hoots and howls filled the woods, frightening the creatures of Sherwood Forest, Robin and Marian included.

Exhausted, they paused for a moment on the crest of a little hill. Before them lay a shallow valley, and beyond that, dimly lit by the rising moon, the rocky face of a cliff.

"We can't keep running," said Robin. Despite a chill in the air, he was drenched in sweat. "And we can't stay put either."

"That doesn't leave us many choices," said Marian.

"My father is going to be worried sick. We promised to be home by dark."

"And we would have been, too, if it hadn't been for the Sheriff," said Marian. "We'll explain everything when we get back. I'm sure he'll understand."

"I hope so," said Robin. He looked up into the branches of a big oak. "Maybe we can spend the night in a tree."

Marian squinted across the valley. "I've got another idea. There's a cave cut into that cliff over there. See it?"

"Yeah, I think so."

"We'd be safer there than in a tree."

"You're probably right," said Robin. "Unless it's full of wolves."

Marian cocked an ear and listened.

"The wolves are far away, hunting deer, or maybe

even the Sheriff." She motioned with her hand. "Follow me."

With the full moon to guide their way, Robin and Marian scrambled down a slope and cut across the little valley to where a jagged cave entrance had been punched into the rock as if by a giant fist.

"I wish I'd brought my bow," whispered Robin as they crept up to the entrance on their hands and knees. "I always feel better about walking into a strange place when there's an arrow strung into my bow."

Marian raised a hand to quiet her friend, then poked her head into the cave. "I don't see anything," she whispered. "I'm going in."

Robin glanced back at the forest, then followed her inside, still on hands and knees.

Silently they shuffled forward across a floor of hard-packed dirt punctuated by rough stones. A heavy scent of old smoke hung in the air, telling them there had been a fire in the cave once. That meant there were probably no wolves lurking in the shadows, but there could be humans, a far more dangerous foe.

"I've got a bad feeling about this place," said Robin.

Marian's eyes could barely make out the rocky walls, a pile of twigs and branches, as well as the remains of a fire pit. "Look at this," she said, picking up a long piece of bone shattered at the end. She rose to her feet and looked around. "Someone must have camped here."

Robin got to his feet and took the bone from Marian.

A gust of wind came rattling into the cave like a spirit, and Marian and Robin both shuddered.

"Anybody here?" called Robin, swinging the bone like a sword. "Speak up if you are. We're armed!" he lied.

When no one answered, he relaxed a little and stepped deeper into the cave, still swinging the bone. "Leave now and our soldiers won't harm you!" he called, his voice growing louder and bolder the more certain he became that the cave was deserted. "I am Robert of Locksley, and if you try to fight me, you'll see that I'm as able with my sword as I am with my bow!" He swung the bone again, higher this time, clipping the cave ceiling, as well as something else: a family of bats.

"Eeeee—eeeech! Eeeee-eeech!" the bats screeched, dropping from the ceiling like a swarm of giant flies. It all happened so quickly Robin only had time to scream. There may have been only ten or twenty of them, but to Robin it seemed like hundreds. Their black bodies were everywhere, flapping wildly, swirling about, their bare wings beating at the air like muffled drums. "Eeeee-yyiiii!" He slapped at the bats as they tumbled past, screeching out of the cave and into the night.

"Whew," said Marian, shivering from the horror. "That was awful. Thank goodness they're all gone."

"Don't be so certain," said Robin, dusting off his hands. "I think I can still hear them squeaking."

Marian cocked an ear toward the back of the cave. Robin was right. Something was alive in the shadows. Something making an awful, whining sound. It was no bat though. She knew that much. It was something else. Something worse.

CHAPTER TEN

SOMETHING WORSE

"What is it?" whispered Robin.

"Shhhh," said Marian. "Listen."

Robin halted. The two stood still and silent. The sound came again.

"A-weeeee, weeee, a-weeeee, ya."

Alone in the blackness, Marian thought of her father, far away in the Sheriff's dungeon. At least she could turn and run from the nightmare. Her father had no such choice.

"A-weeee, glup, glam, a-weeee, hulp." The noise came again.

Robin leaned forward and peered into the blackness, shielding his eyes with his hand as though that might help somehow.

"Glup, hulp, hulpa."

"That doesn't sound like any animal I know," said Robin.

"Hello! Who's there?" shouted Marian.

"A-weeee! Halap!"

"Help?" asked Marian.

"Halap! Halap!"

"Someone's back there," said Marian. "Someone in trouble."

"Halap!"

Marian moved cautiously forward.

"Be careful!" said Robin.

The cave grew blacker, then blacker still. Guided by the muffled words, Marian ducked low and put her hands before her as though trying to part the darkness like a curtain.

"I'm coming," she called softly.

"Hulap-heeelp."

Suddenly her fingers found something hairy. She let out a gasp and drew back her hand. At first she thought she'd found an animal. Then she realized it was a man. She'd blundered into his stubbly beard.

"You don't know how glad I am you're here," he said as she pulled off the cloth that had been gagging him. "Untie us."

"Us?"

"A-wee too."

Now that Marian's eyes has adjusted to the darkness of the moonlit cave, she could make out the forms of two men sitting on the ground of the cave. They were tied back to back, their hands bound together by a single rope. Marian removed his gag as well.

"Are you all right?" Robin was alongside her now, shrouded in the darkness.

"Untie us," demanded one of the men. His voice was high and whiny. Marian thought she'd heard it before.

"In a moment," said Marian. "First tell us who you are and what you're doing here."

"Untie us," the man repeated. "Our feet are bound. Our hands too. Quickly. They could be back any minute."

"Back here? Who?"

"The thieves," said the other man in a thin voice. "Do you want us all to be killed? Believe me, they'd sooner slit your throats as look at you."

"They would? And me without my bow," said Robin, cursing his bad luck.

Marian was almost certain she'd heard both the voices before. "What do these thieves want with you?"

"Untie us, please."

Marian snapped her fingers. "Those voices! It's Norman and Simon!"

"The Sheriff's tax collectors?" said Robin.

"Alas, that's a job we no longer have," came Norman's voice. "And who might you be?"

"Marian and Robin," said Marian.

"Marian!" exclaimed Simon. "You're the girl with the amazing pig. Why, he predicted our fate precisely. The Sheriff fired us not two days ago! And look at us now. Did he not say we'd be robbed by thieves?"

"Did you bring the pig with you?" asked Norman. "Perhaps he can tell us where those cutthroats are."

Marian rolled her eyes. Simon and Norman were as stupid as ever. "What in heaven's name would thieves ever want with the likes of you two?"

"They want what's in our heads," said Simon.

"That can't be much," muttered Robin.

"Aye, but it is," said Norman, "for they think we know where the Sheriff keeps his gold."

"But we don't," said Simon.

"Why didn't you just make something up?" suggested Marian.

"They won't free us until they have the Sheriff's

gold," said Norman. "If they come back empty-handed, we're dead."

"Sounds like you're dead either way," said Marian.

"Perhaps we should get going," said Robin. All this talk of death was making him very uncomfortable.

"Please, you can't just leave us here," said Simon.

Robin sighed. "No, I suppose we can't."

"Then cut us loose," said Norman. "Do so and we'll be eternally grateful."

"We'll pay you back any way we can," said Simon. "We're on your side now, not the Sheriff's. Quickly now."

Marian searched in the dark and found the rope binding Norman's hands. She fumbled with the knot for a minute, but couldn't loosen it.

"They've tied you up tighter than a new pair of boots." She pulled on the rope some more, then finally gave up in exasperation.

"Don't you have a knife?" asked Norman desperately.

"Sorry," said Marian, still struggling to free the men. "Heavens! Whoever tied you up knows his knots. Now, if I had a little light perhaps I could—"

As though on cue, the entrance of the cave was suddenly flooded with light.

"It's them!" gasped Norman.

"We're all goners now," moaned Simon.

"The knot. Hurry!" cried Norman.

"I...I can't," whispered Marian just as two men, each holding a flaming torch, came stomping into the cave. Marian and Robin fell back into the shadows and hid behind a boulder.

One of the men, a huge fellow with a tangled black beard covering most of his face and a long, jagged scar running from his left temple along his cheek, grunted and threw the bodies of three rabbits onto the ground.

"Pinch! Cook us up some supper!" he growled, turning to his friend, a thin, red-headed, long-nosed man with a scruffy red beard. He dropped a bow along with a quiver of arrows at his feet. Then he took a large knife from his belt and tossed it on the ground next to Pinch. "You'd better start on the rabbits," he said. "I'll see if I can't loosen the tongues of those two sorry souls in the back."

"If anyone can get someone to talk, it's you, Slash," said Pinch, the thin man. He laughed. "And if they won't talk for you, let me have a chance at them. I'd like to find out if it's as easy to skin a tax collector as it is a rabbit."

Pinch bent over, swept some wood into a pile, and

started a fire with the burning torch. He then picked up the knife and began to skin the rabbits.

Slash picked up a bucket of water and came toward Norman and Simon, chuckling quietly to himself from behind his wild black beard. "I imagine you boys must have developed a powerful thirst by now," Slash said as he dipped a hand into the water and flicked drops at Norman and Simon. "Ready to talk yet? How about some information in exchange for a little sip?"

"We told you. We don't know anything," said Norman. "Do you think the Sheriff would share those kinds of secrets with his tax collectors?"

"I suspect you placed the goods in the vault yourselves," Slash said. He paused, peered closely at Norman and Simon, and wrinkled his brow. "Someone's been here!"

Marian and Robin held their breath, peering from behind the boulder in the shadows. The flickering firelight lit the fat man's face with an eerie glow.

"Answer me!" demanded Slash. "Who removed those gags?"

CHAPTER ELEVEN

SLASH'S KNIFE

Without warning, Slash wheeled, took a few steps back, then seized a burning stick from the fire and waved it in Norman's face.

"I'm asking you one last time. Was anybody here?"

Marian shuddered. She knew that Norman and Simon were stupid enough to admit the truth and condemn them to death.

"The cloth just fell off," said Norman at last. "No one helped us."

"You may be good thieves, but you're not very handy with a gag," said Simon. He laughed.

"Bah!" snorted Slash, withdrawing the burning stick.

Pinch had just skewered the three rabbits with sharpened sticks and held them over the fire. The meat had already begun to sizzle and pop. After a short while the cave was filled with the sweet smell of supper. Marian's mouth was watering with hunger. She wanted more than anything to ask for a bite of the rabbit, but she wisely held her tongue.

Norman and Simon weren't nearly so shy.

"Have some mercy," begged Norman. "Give us a drop of water and a scrap of that meat. We haven't had food nor drink all day. Not since you snatched us on the road."

"We aren't particular. Even a piece of bone would do," said Simon.

Slash took the knife Pinch used on the rabbits, wiped off the blade on his sleeve, and came lumbering over to the tax collectors. He had to stoop to avoid the low ceiling.

"So it's a bit of supper you want?" he asked, slowly tracing the track of his scar with the blade of his knife.

Norman eyed the knife warily. "Just a bite of food and a sip of water. That's not too much to ask, is it?"

"We'll give you a whole rabbit and a bucket of water if you'll just tell us where the Sheriff keeps his goods. That's not too much to ask either, now is it?"

Marian heard Simon moan. "But we told you a thousand times. We don't know where he keeps his gold. If we did, don't you think we would have talked by now?"

Slash knelt down in front of Simon and touched his nose with the tip of his knife. "I think all you care about is protecting that no-good Sheriff."

Simon crinkled his nose. "Why would we want to do that? The Sheriff fired us. That's why we were tramping along the road when you found us. Otherwise we'd have been riding in a cart."

"We hate the Sheriff," added Norman.

"Slash!" called Pinch. "Bring that knife over here and cut me off a piece of meat."

"Is it cooked yet?" asked Slash, rising.

"It's warm," Pinch answered. "Let's eat."

"What about us?" asked Norman.

"I've got a feeling we'll be skinning you next," Slash said, wiggling the knife in Norman's face.

Robin shivered so hard at the man's last words that he shook loose a rock from the cave walls.

"Eh? What's that?" asked Slash, pointing with the knife.

Marian's heart began pounding so loudly that she was afraid it might give them away.

There was a moment's silence. Marian held her

breath. At last Pinch said, "All you heard was the bats. Now, are we going to eat or not?"

Marian sighed with relief and the thieves began their merry feast. They ate two of the rabbits, then washed them down with great gulps of water from the bucket. After they'd spit out the last of the bones and wiped their greasy hands on their filthy woolen breeches, Pinch brought out a leather pouch and passed it over to Slash.

"Here you go, Slash," he said. "Have yourself a bit of wine. We'll celebrate our good fortune."

Slash laughed, then lifted the pouch to his lips and squirted a stream of wine into his throat. "Ahh," he said, wiping off his beard with the back of his hand. "This has been a good day, my friend. Usually a few pennies is the most we ever snatch from travelers on the road to Nottingham. But today we nabbed ourselves a fortune."

"I told you, we know nothing," said Norman through his cracked, dry lips. "How about sharing that last rabbit with us," he whined. "If you don't want to eat it, then—"

"Shut up!" snarled Pinch.

Marian could hear Norman sniffle, then start to cry.

If either of the thieves heard him, they didn't seem to care. For the next hour, the two exchanged crude jokes and nightmarish tales of robbery and murder as they passed the wine skin back and forth.

Marian and Robin stayed still and silent, certain they'd be discovered at any moment. From time to time, the flickering flames lit their faces, but they were never spotted. Perhaps it was because the thieves believed Norman's explanation about the gag and so had no reason to suspect anyone else was in the cave. Perhaps it was the poor light. Perhaps it was the wine. Whatever the reason, Marian was thankful for it.

Gradually the lateness of the hour and the wine began to take their toll. Pinch was first to surrender to sleep, curling up by the fire like a dog, his head cradled in his elbow.

"Stoke up the fire," he mumbled before drifting off. "I wouldn't want the wolves to pay us a visit."

Slash belched in reply, then threw some wood into the pit. The fire flared up anew, suddenly illuminating the boulder Marian and Robin were hiding behind.

However, they had nothing to fear. For no sooner had Slash finished with the fire, he pulled off his boots, lay down, and began snoring away like a fat bear in winter.

Robin and Marian remained quiet for a few more minutes until they were certain Pinch was snoring as well. Then they tiptoed out of their hiding place and started for freedom.

"Hey, wait!" whispered Norman as they passed by. "You can't just leave us here."

"We'll be killed for sure," said Simon.

"Your ropes are too tight," said Robin. "Sorry."

"But that bearded fellow had a knife," said Norman, his voice a bare whisper. "Cut us loose with that."

Robin looked over at the sleeping men. He could see Slash's knife clearly, jammed under his belt.

"Please," begged Norman.

"All right," said Robin. He drew in a deep breath and stepped forward, but before he could reach for the knife, Marian was at his side. She gently touched his elbow.

"Let me do it," she whispered. "After all, I'm the expert pickpocket here."

"That's the girl," whispered Norman. "We'll be eternally grateful."

"Eternally," agreed Simon.

Marian blew lightly on her fingers, then took two silent steps forward. The two thieves had been sleeping restlessly, turning from side to side in their drunken slumber, and as Marian approached Pinch, he rolled into the half-filled water bucket, nearly spilling the contents onto his friend. Robin snatched it out of the way just before it toppled over and set it safely out of the way.

"The fools," he whispered. "It's a miracle they haven't tumbled into the fire and cooked themselves to a crisp."

Stepping lightly over Pinch, Marian bent over Slash and studied the sleeping figure. His bearded, scarred cheek was pressed into the earth, and his tongue was visible at the corner of his mouth. She bent closer still, then suddenly pulled back. As hard as it was to believe, he smelled even worse than he looked.

The knife handle was clearly visible above his belt. Silent as a feather dropping through fog, Marian lowered her hand and grasped the handle with two fingers. Behind her, Pinch grunted and rolled over. She looked up. His eyes were still closed. Immediately she returned her attention to Slash, tightened her grip, and then Whop! in a single motion she slipped the knife out from under his belt and brought it high over her head.

"Arrrgh!" he grunted. His hand shot out from under his cheek like a striking snake. "Arrrgh." He grabbed at an invisible foe and came up with a handful of air.

Marian's heart leapt to her throat. If she had to use the knife, she would. She knew, though, that even with the knife, she wouldn't stand a chance against someone as big as the thief.

"Urrrg," he grunted again, rolling over. Marian held her position and waited. Ten seconds went by, then twenty. He didn't move again. Finally he sniffled twice and fell back into a deep sleep. Marian let out a giant sigh. She couldn't remember the last time she'd heard a sound quite so sweet as Slash's snores.

Now there was little time to waste. She tossed the knife gently to land at Robin's feet. The thieves did not hear the quiet thump. A moment later Robin was using the knife to slash the ropes binding Simon's and Norman's hands and feet. Within minutes he'd cut them free.

All this had been done without a word being exchanged. When the silence was finally broken, it was Norman who spoke. "I'm grabbing that last rabbit on the way out," he whispered. He swallowed, then licked his lips. "Simon, you get that water bucket."

"Don't be stupid," whispered Marian. "Do you

want to wake those two up? If you have any sense at all, you'll just tiptoe on out of here without even stopping to breathe."

"Are you saying I've no sense?" said Norman, raising his voice.

"Urrgh!" Slash grunted again and rolled over.

Instinctively, the four of them fell back into the shadows and held their breath. Finally Marian whispered, "See what I mean? Don't stop to pick anything up."

"Speak for yourself," said Robin. "I'm picking up the bow and that quiver of arrows. We're going to need them."

Marian rolled her eyes. "I give up. Let's just go."

Norman and Simon were off before the words had left Marian's mouth. Norman leapt over the sleeping thieves, grabbing the stick with the cooked rabbit. He was out the cave door a second later.

Simon hurried over to the water bucket and picked it up. Unlike his partner, however, he didn't keep going. Instead, he paused to drink. Though he didn't notice what was happening, Robin and Marian did. In his haste to gulp down the water, he was spilling some of it down his chin. It would have been all right had Slash's face not been directly beneath that chin.

Before Robin and Marian had even taken a step, Slash had stirred to life. "Arrrgh!" he growled, raising up his head.

Simon froze in place, the bucket tipped to his lips.

Robin shoved the knife under his belt and took off for the cave entrance.

"Wake up!" Slash bellowed to his friend. Fully awake now, he reached for his knife and found it gone.

Pinch came awake just as Robin shot by.

"What's the...who's the..." he cried, shaking his head.

Marian, trailing Robin, suddenly found herself trapped by Slash. He'd rolled onto his hands and knees and was now lumbering her way like an angry bear.

She swallowed, then gathered her strength and charged. Her hope was that she could run past him before he could react. She was within three feet when he suddenly rose up with a roar.

"Gotcha!" he crowed, clamping her into his huge arms.

Marian looked up. His bloated, scarred face, made all the worse by the shadows from the fire, leered down at her as if she might be his next meal.

"Get up, you blunder-headed fool!" Slash yelled to

Pinch. "Our fortune's just run out the door!"

Robin paused at the cave entrance and looked back. When he saw what had happened to Marian, he gasped and reached for the knife in his belt.

In all the commotion no one had yet noticed Simon still holding the bucket of water. While Slash shouted orders to his partner, Simon quietly set down the bucket and began edging out of the cave, trying his best not to draw any attention. He had very nearly made it to the entrance when Pinch spotted him.

"It's one of the tax collectors!" he yelled.

In a flash Simon was running for the night with Pinch on his heels. Robin let Simon pass, but stepped in front of Pinch and bared the knife.

"Hold it!" he yelled.

Pinch halted in his tracks. "Who are you?" he asked, narrowing his eyes. He looked mightily confused.

For a moment the two eyed each other warily.

"Keep back," said Robin, stabbing at the air with the knife. "I'm not afraid to use this!"

Pinch stepped back, his hands raised. "Give it to me," he said coldly.

Robin gulped. Any battle with outlaws like these he was certain to lose. The knife would be at his own throat long before he could put it to Pinch's. The bow and arrows were still in the cave, but even if he could get to them, they'd do him no good. He'd be jumped before he could ready a single arrow. That left but one weapon within reach, the bucket of water.

"Robin! Help!" cried Marian. He'd never seen her look quite so desperate.

Robin drew in a deep breath and stepped forward, waving the knife like a sword. "Let her go!" he demanded, forcing Pinch back toward the fire.

"Grab him, you fool!" growled Slash. "Can't you see he's only a boy?"

Before either of them could attack, Robin ran into the cave, snatched up the bucket in his free hand, and swung it like a club, splashing bits of water onto Pinch's filthy shirt.

Slash looked out across the fire and laughed. "Do you think you can scare us with that bucket? Go on. Try hitting us with it! Believe me, boy, that bucket will crack long before our heads do!"

Robin didn't doubt that. The two were as iron-headed as bells.

Marian twisted around far enough to catch Robin's eye. He grinned and raised up the bucket. But instead of throwing it at Pinch, he hurled its contents onto the fire.

Psssst! In an instant the flames were extinguished and the cave was plunged into an inky blackness. It was the very moment Marian had been waiting for.

She raised up her boot like a hammer and brought it down squarely on Slash's bare foot. The fool had taken off his boots before going to sleep.

"Ow! Ouch!" he bellowed, releasing Marian as he grabbed for his throbbing toe. "Blast it all! The girl's getting away!"

Marian scrambled over to the cave wall, then scooted sideways all the way out of the cave. Robin took a more direct route, pausing just long enough to grab the bow and quiver of arrows before making his way to safety.

BAM!

"I just smacked one of them with my fist!" Pinch cried out.

"You dolt! That was me!" shouted Slash in reply. "Take this, you idiot!"

POW BAM! WHAP!

A full-blown battle had broken out in the blackness. The two were brawling like wildcats. Robin and Marian waited for a moment outside the cave, enjoying the symphony of curses, shouts, and blows.

"Thanks," said Marian, raising her two fingers. "You saved my life."

"My pleasure," said Robin, returning the salute. "Two forever. Now let's get out of here."

CHAPTER TWELVE

WORDS OF DOOM

Robin and Marian rushed back into the forest. They followed the twisted path through the bushes and trees, barely speaking, eyes and ears alert. No one had to remind them that they were as lost as ever, but trails as big as the one they were on had to lead somewhere. That somewhere, they hoped, was the main road.

Suddenly they heard a sound. "Pssst!"

Marian halted, raising her hand for Robin to do the same.

"What is it?" he whispered.

"A snake, I think," said Marian. "Don't move... Ouch!" Something sharp had just poked her in the side.

"Pssst!"

Marian got stuck again. "Ow!"

"In here!"

"It's us, Norman and Simon." Marian looked down and saw a stick extending from a bush. "We found a great hiding place."

Marian rubbed her side and peered into the tangled brush. She couldn't see a thing.

"You saved us. Let us return the favor," came Norman's voice. "Come. There's plenty of room."

Marian groaned. What choice did she have? She could either run with the wolves or hunker down in a bush with a pair of idiots. It wasn't a hard decision to make. Idiots, at least, didn't bite.

She parted some branches and crawled into the bush. Robin followed. There was a small, hollowed-out area inside, perhaps an old wolf den.

Norman and Simon were waiting, hunched down, sharing the rabbit they'd picked up in the cave. Norman offered Marian and Robin a blackened leg. "Want some supper?"

Robin shook his head no. Marian made a face. The rabbit was now black and cold. She'd sooner eat charcoal. That suited the tax collectors just fine. All the more for them.

For the next hour they talked quietly of many things, including their plans for the future.

"We've heard the town of Canterbury needs new tax collectors," said Simon. "We'll be heading that way at first light."

"And Robin and I will be journeying to Nottingham," said Marian. "In a few days I plan to rescue my father."

"He's in the dungeon," added Robin.

"The Sheriff's dungeon?" said Norman. "No one's ever escaped from there."

"I haven't worked out a plan yet," said Marian. "In the meantime I'll need your help."

Simon gulped. "We owe you a favor, but we can't go back." He put his arms around himself and shivered. "Please, don't ask us to go."

"Don't worry," Marian assured him. "All I need from you is information."

Simon sighed with relief. "Just information?"

"Tell me about the dungeon," said Marian. "We'll do the rest."

"Actually, there's not much to it," said Norman, leaning forward. "We've never been down there."

"You've never been inside?" asked Robin.

"The Sheriff lets only his most trusted soldiers into the dungeon," said Norman. He lowered his voice.

"There are secrets in there that are too terrible to tell, so I've heard."

"What kind of secrets?" asked Robin cautiously.

"I don't know," said Norman. "But there's someone who could quickly give you the answer."

"Really?" said Marian. She brightened. "Who?"

"Why, Timothy the pig, of course," said Norman. "He knows everything. He even predicted we'd lose our jobs and be robbed by bandits!"

"He's smarter than all of us combined," said Simon.

Marian looked at Robin and shook her head. It was clear the tax collectors were not going to be much help.

But she was wrong.

"We're lost," Marian told them. "How do we get to Nottingham?"

"That's easy," said Norman. "When the sun comes up, we'll show you."

And at dawn's first light they led Robin and Marian through the trees a short way to the road.

"I had no idea we were so close all this time," said Robin.

"Actually, we shouldn't be so surprised," said Marian. "Those lazy robbers would never have strayed far from their place of business."

At the mention of the two cutthroats, Simon looked nervously over his shoulder, then cleared his throat. "Well," he said, tipping his hat, "I suppose we should be on our way. Canterbury is a full day's journey."

"Are you sure you don't want to come to Nottingham?" asked Marian. "Your knowledge of the castle could come in handy."

"I'm sure it could," said Norman, "but if the Sheriff catches us in Nottingham, we'll hang for sure." He put one hand on Marian's shoulder and another on Robin's. "Be careful in town today, my friends. If you are captured, you'll hang as well."

Robin winced. "Do you really think so?"

"I'm quite certain," said Norman. He tapped Marian on the nose. "Even your pig will tell you that's the truth."

And with his chilling words still hanging in the air, he turned, waved over his shoulder, and started down the road with Simon at his side.

"Have a safe journey!" yelled Marian.

"And the same to you!" replied Norman, without turning back.

Marian and Robin watched them until they disappeared around a bend. Then they started off in the opposite direction toward Nottingham.

It was a beautiful day. The air was clear and warm. The trees glowed green as emeralds. And the forest itself was rich with the scent of pine and the sweet sounds of birdsong. Unfortunately, neither of them noticed any of this. That's because their minds were on other matters, including the fact that they might soon be hung. So absorbed were they with these awful thoughts that they very nearly blundered into one of the Sheriff's soldiers.

They came upon him suddenly, just as they rounded a sharp turn. Fortunately, his back was to them at the time. He was busy posting a piece of parchment to a tree. His horse, which was tethered across the road, looked up and whinnied. The soldier turned, but before he could turn all the way around, Robin and Marian dived into the trees.

They stayed hidden, their hearts pounding, until the soldier finished his work and rode off toward the castle. Then they walked over to the tree to examine the notice he'd posted.

"It's all about the grand festival to be held at Nottingham just three days hence," said Robin. "There will be food and dancing and even a puppet play. It's the one the Sheriff was talking about back in the clearing."

Marian, who skipped toward the bottom of the notice, said, "And look, they are promising to have a hanging as a special treat."

Robin stopped reading and asked, "Does it say who is to be hung?"

Marian gasped. "It does!"

"Who?"

"My father," she whispered.

CHAPTER THIRTEEN

THREE DAYS

Three days. Three days until she was to be orphaned. Usually, in a crisis Marian's mind would have been hard at work on a solution. But not this time. The sight of her father's name on the poster had put her into a daze.

"We'll get him out," said Robin as they tramped down the road. "You'll see. We'll find a way."

Marian turned and eyed him blankly. It was as if someone had opened a spigot and drained away her spirit.

Robin patted the bow he'd picked up in the cave. "I'll cut the hangman's rope with an arrow if I have to," he said, trying to cheer her.

Marian wiped a tear from her eye and lowered her head.

"Sorry," said Robin. "Maybe it's better if we don't talk about it."

And they didn't. Not for hours. But late that afternoon, when they reached the little stone cottage of Thomas the Woodsman, it was the first thing out of her old friend's mouth.

"Marian! I'm so sorry," he said, greeting her at the door. "I just learned your father is to die. Dreadful. Terrible news indeed."

"Poor, poor, child," said Mary, Thomas's wife. She wrapped her plump arms around Marian and held her close.

Marian buried her head in Mary's chest and sobbed. Mary had been almost like a mother to her ever since her own mother had disappeared.

They held each other for a long time, while Robin stood silently by, staring at the floor and nervously shuffling his feet. He looked up just as Mary reached over and gave his cheek a pinch.

"Goodness, boy, you're thin as a reed. When was the last time you ate?"

"I can't remember," said Robin. "More than a day, I'd guess."

"Then both of you take a seat at the table," she

said, letting go of Marian. "We'll warm your bellies with some nice hot broth."

"Robin, I'll get word to your father that you're all right," said Thomas. "He was here this morning asking about you."

"I'm afraid I've caused him a lot of worry," said Robin. "I appreciate your offer to pass along the news that I'm well."

Before long Marian and Robin were gulping down Mary's soup. They each had three bowls, and would have had more had they been greedy. But they both knew how poor Mary and Thomas were, and if they ate another helping, they'd be taking food from their hosts' own mouths.

After the meal, with nightfall settling over the forest, Marian and Robin lay down on straw mattresses. It had been nearly as long since they'd rested as it had been since they'd eaten. They fell quickly into a long, deep sleep, not awakening until the next day at dawn.

"Good morning," said Mary as soon as she saw them stir.

"You slept clean through the night," said Thomas. He'd just come in with an armful of wood for the fire. "Can we get you something to eat?"

Marian combed her golden hair with her fingers, then stood up and dusted the straw from her dress. For a moment she seemed confused. She'd slept in so many different places the last few nights that it took her a moment to orient herself.

"Thomas and I have been talking," said Mary. "You know, about the hanging."

The hanging! The words suddenly brought Marian to her senses. She looked out the window at the new day and moaned. "Two days," she whispered to herself. "Just two days left."

"You'll always have a home here with us," said Mary. "As long as Thomas and I are alive, you'll never be an orphan."

"You're very kind," said Marian. She straightened. "But I have no intention of becoming an orphan of any kind." She shot a glance at Robin. He'd just gotten up and was stretching his arms toward the ceiling. "My father isn't going to hang. If I have to snatch him off the gallows with my bare hands, I swear that's what I'll do."

"You can't be serious," said Mary.

"Any attempt to free your father would be suicide," said Thomas. "Why, you'd end up in the dungeon yourself."

"Or hung," said Mary. "It's too late to save your father. Please, my dear, at least try to save yourself." She wrinkled her brow with worry. "Oh, you're so much like your mother."

"That suits me just fine. Like her, I'm prepared to die if necessary."

Two days! To Marian the time seemed infernally short. The way people talked about the Sheriff's dungeon, she would need an army to free her father. Unfortunately, Marian had neither an army nor the time to recruit one. Or did she? Norman and Simon had mentioned that the dungeon held some terrible secrets. She had an idea what they might possibly be. The secrets, she thought, might just help her free her father.

By the afternoon she had a plan.

"I'll need your help," she told Thomas. "I want to make sure all our friends are in Nottingham tomorrow—Anne the Seamstress, Elizabeth the Innkeeper, Christopher the Hunter, everyone. Can I count on you to pass the word?"

Thomas nodded. "I owe your father many favors. It's the least I can do."

"You won't be trying anything foolish now, will you?" asked Mary.

"Foolish? Me?" said Marian. She smiled. "Don't worry. I don't plan to make any mistakes. My father's life depends on it."

"Our lives depend on it," said Robin. He shook his head. "I hope you know what you're doing."

That night Robin could barely sleep. He was certain the coming day was going to be his last on earth. On the other hand, Marian hardly stirred. In fact, she might have slept through the morning had Robin not shaken her awake just after dawn.

"Please," said Mary as she came into the little room, "don't go. It's not too late to save yourselves."

"We've made up our minds," said Marian firmly. "I'm sorry, Mary, but our next stop is Nottingham and the Sheriff's gallows."

No one in the room doubted the truth of Marian's words. One way or another Thomas and Mary knew that the two friends were heading for the gallows. What no one knew was whether they were going to end up there as rescuers or as condemned prisoners.

CHAPTER FOURTEEN

THE DUNGEON

Though it was early, a number of travelers had already passed by the woodsman's cottage on the road to Nottingham. Festivals, especially free ones, were rare events in the kingdom, and just about everyone in Sherwood Forest was expected to attend.

"Here, wear this," said Mary, wrapping a scarf around Marian's golden hair. "When you get to town, be sure to pull the end over your face." She dropped a few pennies into Marian's hand. "Buy yourself some food. You'll need all your strength if you hope to free your father."

Thomas loaned Robin his cloak. It was too big, but that was all right, for it helped to conceal both his face and the bow and quiver strapped to his back.

"We'll be along later," said Thomas. He gently

squeezed Robin's shoulder. "Be careful now."

"We will," said Marian. She looked up into Mary's eyes, then threw herself into her arms. They hugged each other tightly. Mary's eyes watered. A tear found its way down Marian's cheek. It went unsaid, but they both knew they might never see each other again.

Finally, with the rising sun just about to crest the pines, Robin and Marian set out on the road to Nottingham. Lost in their thoughts, they moved swiftly, acknowledging the people they passed with only a quick nod of the head or a curt, "Good day."

By the time they reached the town, the sun was straight overhead and the day had turned hot and dry. Beneath his woolen hood, Robin had begun to sweat, but he didn't dare remove the cloak. There was a price on his head, and in those difficult times, when a gold coin could buy much, he didn't dare trust anyone.

They joined a large family of ragged peasants and moved past the soldiers at the village gate. The soldiers eyed them closely but apparently didn't recognize them. They weren't stopped or searched.

Once inside, they melted into the festival crowd, pausing to look around at the thrilling sights of the festival itself: brightly colored tents offering wondrous goods from the far corners of the world, bits of silk from China, stoneware from the coast of France, and rings and pins and candlesticks from the finest silversmiths in far-off London. The shouts of the merchants mingled in the air with the luscious scents of pork, chicken, and potatoes sizzling on spits. Jugglers and mimes competed for attention, while small children ran around their parents or played hide-and-seek between the tents.

When they arrived at the center of the square, Marian and Robin were met by the sight of a newly constructed gallows, complete with four hangman's ropes positioned over four trap doors.

"I wish Timothy were here to predict the future," said Marian. "I can't bear to think of what might happen."

Robin reached back and patted the bow hidden beneath his cloak. "Don't worry. I've planned for the future."

Marian smiled thinly from behind her scarf, then glanced up at a pair of giant stone gargoyles cemented above the entrance to Nottingham Castle. The gargoyles stared back through bulging eyes. Their open, toothless mouths seemed to be taunting her, daring her to enter the castle. A few soldiers were standing on the stairs, talking casually among themselves. Beyond them was the castle door, and beyond it, somewhere, was her father.

Just about everyone turned out for the festival. Marian recognized dozens of faces. Mary and Thomas had done their job well. All their friends were there—people who lived on her father's estate and on the estate of Robin's father. She had known most of them since she was a child. Among them, Marian spotted Anne the Seamstress and Christopher the Hunter. She also saw Robin's father, the Earl of Locksley. He looked worried, but they did not approach him, knowing that he would send them home immediately. Marian saw soldiers in the crowd as well, and even some old enemies.

"Well, well, look who's here," said Marian, pointing. "There, talking to the silversmith."

"It's Slash!" said Robin, spotting the big, bearded robber they hadn't seen since the cave. "I guess he and Pinch must have finished their fight."

"Indeed," said Marian. "In fact, there's Pinch himself, rat's nest beard and all. While Slash is distracting the silversmith, Pinch is about to steal a trinket from that poor man's booth."

Sure enough, the stealthy Pinch had his grubby

hand wrapped around a silver candlestick.

"We ought to warn the silversmith," said Robin.

"No need," said Marian. "Look. One of the Sheriff's soldiers has also spotted the thief."

Sure enough, a squat, red-faced soldier was striding toward Pinch, waving his sword above his head.

"Thieves!" he screamed. "Thieves beneath the Sheriff's own castle!"

All faces turned to the soldier. "Thieves!" he bellowed, plowing into the crowd, the sword raised above his head. "The silversmith's being robbed!"

The silversmith himself looked around, as surprised as anyone else by the news. When he saw the thief about to steal his goods, he shouted and grabbed Pinch by the wrist.

"I've got him!" he yelled.

"More like the other way around. I've got you," snarled Pinch, punctuating his words by whapping the silversmith on the head with the candlestick. The silversmith slumped to the ground.

"Let's go!" cried Slash, and a moment later they took off into the crowd with half a dozen men in pursuit.

"Halt! Stop those thieves!" someone shouted, pointing at the fleeing men. Within seconds every soldier in the square had joined in the chase. The festival-goers scattered out of the way like leaves before the wind. Those who couldn't move fast enough were knocked sprawling. A bucket of eggs was overturned. Slash picked one up and hurled it at a pursuer, splattering him with sticky yellow yolk.

"Don't let them through the gate!" yelled a soldier.

A cageful of pigeons was upended. The wooden bars snapped, and three birds squeezed out and flapped away. The thieves leapt over a small child, ducked under a tent, and moments later emerged from the other side.

"Get them!" cried the silversmith, having finally regained his senses.

Robin and Marian were so enjoying the scene, they didn't realize that the chase had suddenly turned back their way.

"Here they come!" someone yelled, and a moment later Pinch and Slash came sprinting by in a blur, knocking over a giant pot of pea soup as they passed. Before Robin and Marian could get out of the way, they found themselves in a sea of slippery soup, along with a squad of the Sheriff's soldiers.

"Whoa!" yelled Robin, trying to keep his balance.

"Oh no!" cried Marian, her legs churning.

"Help!" yelled one of the soldiers, going down.

"Watch out!" yelled another.

Bam! Splash! Wham! Everyone went down in a tangle of legs and arms and soup.

Luckily, Robin and Marian landed on top of a pile of soldiers, so they didn't get wet. Unluckily, Marian found herself staring into the face of one of those soldiers.

"Why, it's the magistrate's daughter!" he blubbered, seizing her by the wrist.

"And young Locksley as well!" cried another, grabbing Robin by the scruff of the neck.

Robin and Marian fought back, trying to wriggle free. But their struggles were in vain. Robin wished he could get to the bow strapped to his back, but for the moment, he was relieved the soldiers hadn't yet discovered it.

"Get up!" commanded a tall soldier, standing nearby. He pointed with his sword. "Take the traitors to the dungeon! The Sheriff will be glad to see them, I'm sure."

"I wish I could say I was going to be glad to see him," muttered Marian as she was being roughly hauled to her feet.

"I get the feeling this wasn't part of your plan," said Robin.

"Not exactly," said Marian just as someone gave them a poke and marched them off to the castle.

"Marian! Robin!" cried Anne the Seamstress as they were making their way through the crowd. "What are they going to do to you?"

Marian turned to Anne and forced a smile. "We're not done for yet," she said. "Don't let any of our friends go home. This isn't over."

Just before they passed through the huge castle door, Marian glanced up for a last look at the blue sky, then turned to her friend. "Two forever," she said, holding up her fingers.

Robin returned the salute. "Two forever," he vowed.

Neither of them had ever been inside the castle before, and at first they found themselves awestruck by the building's sheer size. Before them, a massive stone and wood staircase wound its way to the upper floors. Huge red tapestries depicting scenes of battle were draped on the walls, while above them, a heavy iron chandelier fitted with candles hung suspended from a chain that disappeared into the upper reaches of the castle. Unfortunately, the entryway was all they were going to see. The soldiers were in no mood to conduct a tour.

"Get a move on!" ordered one of the soldiers, slapping Marian, then Robin, on the back of the head. "The dungeon is waiting."

The soldiers shoved them down the long hallway, passing beneath the stern gazes of a dozen noblemen and women whose portraits were suspended on the gray walls. At the end of the hall was a rough wooden door, and beyond that, a narrow stone staircase leading down into the darkness. A draft of damp air, heavy with the odor of decay, came up from below and forced Marian to put a hand to her face.

"Whew," she said.

"Better get used to it," said one of the soldiers. He laughed, then gave Marian a little push. "Hurry now. The rats and the bugs can't wait to meet you."

At the bottom of the stairs, they arrived at a dank, low-ceilinged, windowless room lit dimly by a torch set into a stone wall. Marian strained her eyes and looked around. Suddenly a rat skittered from the shadows and Robin jumped.

A soldier laughed.

"My heavens," gasped Marian. Her eyes had finally adjusted to the dark. "There are people everywhere."

Marian had expected to find people down in the

dungeon, but not nearly so many. Or in such horrible condition. Scores of them were chained to the walls like dogs. Some were bound by their legs and feet, others by their arms. All that protected most of them from the cold stone floor was a thin layer of filthy straw. The dim torchlight turned their hollow-eyed faces into pale skulls. Someone in the corner was moaning softly. Otherwise all was silent.

"Father!" cried Marian. "Are you here?"

"Over here," came a voice. "I've been waiting for you."

"Father?" said Marian, though the man didn't sound at all like her father.

A moment later the man stepped from the shadows and smiled.

Marian very nearly fainted. It was the Sheriff of Nottingham.

CHAPTER FIFTEEN

THE DUNGEON'S SECRET

"Maid Marian and Robin of Locksley," said the Sheriff. "I was delighted to hear my men had captured you. I figured you wouldn't want to miss the hanging."

"Release my father," said Marian coldly. "You have no right to hold him."

The Sheriff laughed. He stroked his pointed black beard and smiled thinly. "You're hardly in a position to be making demands, don't you think?"

"I think otherwise!" shouted Robin. In a single motion he reached beneath his shirt and undid his bow. A second later he'd fitted it with an arrow and leveled it at the Sheriff. "We appreciate your hospitality," he said sarcastically, "but I'm afraid we can't stay. Now if you'll release Marian's father, we'll be on our way."

In his haste Robin had forgotten about the Sheriff's

soldiers. Now, suddenly, he was aware of someone at his side. He turned and caught sight of torchlight glinting off a soldier's silver breastplate.

WHAP! Something smacked Robin on the side of the head. "Oooof!" he moaned, dropping his bow. WHAM! He was hit again, and this time he crumpled to the floor like a rag doll.

"Robin!" cried Marian.

A moment later, WHAP! she was hit too, and the world went black.

Marian had no idea how long she remained unconscious, but when she woke up, she discovered enough time had passed for someone to chain her leg to the wall. Robin was chained next to her, moaning softly and rubbing his head.

"What...what happened?" he asked.

"We got knocked out," said Marian.

She looked around the dimly lit room, searching for her father. Part of her hoped she wouldn't find him in such an awful place. The walls were covered with black soot from the torches, and insects and rats were scurrying about through the straw, as though the ground beneath their feet were on fire. Most of the people chained to the walls looked as though their years of confinement had driven them mad. Some were babbling to themselves, but most were simply sitting, half-dead, staring out at the darkness. More than a few of them looked familiar, old friends long gone though not forgotten. The woman on her other side, whose long, soot-blackened hair was as matted as an old rug, reached out and patted her head.

"What is your name, child?" the woman asked hoarsely.

"Marian." She eyed the woman suspiciously.

"Marian! Are you all right?" someone called from across the way.

Marian gasped and squinted into the darkness. "Father!"

"I wish you hadn't come," he said.

"I couldn't let them hang you," said Marian.

"Is it better that you hang too?" asked her father.

"He...he wants to hang Marian?" said Robin.

"And you too," said Marian's father. "Stealing from the Sheriff is an offense punishable by death, so says the Sheriff."

Robin gulped, then immediately began searching for his bow, but it was nowhere to be found.

The woman beside Marian said, "My dear girl," and

touched her hair with her thin fingers.

Marian moved away from her toward her father.

"It could have been just me. Now four of us will die," said Marian's father.

"The Sheriff can't hang us. We're too young," said Marian. "Even he isn't that cruel."

"But of course he is," said her father.

Marian turned her face to the sooty wall and groaned. She knew it was the truth.

"Marian," moaned the woman.

Marian squinted. Something about the woman was vaguely familiar. Her face was worn and dirty, but Marian thought that she'd seen that spark in the woman's eyes before.

"What do you mean four of us will die?" she asked her father. "There're only Robin and me and you. Who is the…"

Marian's words caught in her mouth. She turned back to the woman and studied her again. The woman managed a weak smile. Marian gasped, then began to cry and smile at the same time.

"Mother, you're alive!"

CHAPTER SIXTEEN

THE HANGMAN'S NOOSE

"I...I thought you'd died," cried Marian.

"I was kidnapped while out hunting," said Marian's mother, Lady Eleanor. She gestured around the dreary room. "Most of these people are guilty of the same crime, objecting to the Sheriff's laws. He holds us secretly, for he knows the people would rise up if they knew their loved ones had been taken. The old snake can't stand dissent, especially when it comes from a woman."

"And even more when that woman is a girl," said Marian.

Lady Eleanor stroked her daughter's golden hair. "I never thought I'd see you again," she said, choking out the words.

Marian couldn't stop shaking her head. "You're alive, really alive."

"Oh, sweet Marian," said her mother. "We'll never be apart again."

"Never," said Marian. "As long as I'm alive, I'll—"

Just then she was interrupted by a tremendous clatter on the stairs. A moment later three soldiers, their armor reflecting the dull torchlight, clamored into the dungeon.

"It's time," said one, pointing his sword.

"For what?" said Robin.

"For the hanging, of course," said the soldier. "There's a crowd outside expecting to see a show." He leaned down until his red, puffy nose was practically touching Marian's face. "You ought to feel honored, young lady. You're the main attraction."

"No, please," begged Lady Eleanor. "Don't take her. Take me."

"Don't worry. We haven't forgotten you," said the soldier, undoing Marian's chains. "The carpenter built the gallows for four. We wouldn't want his work to go to waste, now would we?"

Marian kicked at the soldier's knee, but her foot slammed harmlessly into his metal shin guard. He laughed and cuffed her on the side of the head.

"Ouch!" she cried.

"Marian!" said Robin.

Marian turned. Robin raised his fingers.

Marian swallowed, then touched his fingers with her own. "Two forever," she whispered.

"Tie up their hands!" ordered the soldier. "Then march them to the gallows."

Though Marian, Robin, Lady Eleanor, and Geoffrey the Magistrate all struggled, they were no match for the soldiers. One by one they were unchained and their hands tied behind their backs. Then they were marched out of the dungeon and shoved up the stairs at the point of the soldiers' swords.

When Geoffrey and Eleanor stepped into the light of day after so many days of darkness, they were momentarily blinded. Marian and Robin, however, could see perfectly well that the Sheriff himself was waiting on the steps to greet them.

"I plan to teach the entire kingdom a lesson today," he said, addressing the crowd.

"What lesson would that be?" asked Marian's mother, recognizing the Sheriff's voice. "That only cowards hang children?"

A murmur went up from the crowd. Marian was glad to see that the years of imprisonment hadn't dimmed her mother's spirit.

"Marian and Robin are not children," replied the Sheriff coldly. "They're traitors." He slowly stroked his beard and raised a single eyebrow. "Let it be clear to one and all that the penalty for mocking the Sheriff of Nottingham is death."

"My only regret is that I didn't mock you more," said Marian defiantly.

"That's my girl," said Marian's mother.

"Impudent fools!" The Sheriff gestured at the prisoners. "Hang the lot of them!"

Robin looked at the crowd swarming about the gallows and felt his knees go weak. Despite his fears, he lifted his head high. He knew what he had done was right, and he was prepared to pay the price.

"Move along now," said the soldiers, punctuating the command with pokes of their swords. "Step lively now. We wouldn't want to keep the hangman waiting."

"I don't mind if he waits," mumbled Robin, starting down the steps.

As soon as the people in the crowd saw the grim procession heading their way, they began shouting and yelling and waving their fists.

From a distance Marian couldn't tell whether they

were excited for the show to begin or whether they were protesting the hangings. However, when they got closer, Marian could see that most of the people in the square were on their side. And as they mounted the crude steps leading to the gallows, the shouts grew ever more intense. All along, her plan had been to rally the people to rise up against the Sheriff. What had not been part of the plan was that she would have to deliver the speech with a noose around her neck.

"Let them go!" some people were shouting.

"What crimes have those children committed?" demanded Anne the Seamstress.

"Robin, my son!" cried the Earl of Locksley, reaching out for his boy. He tried to follow him up the steps but was rudely pushed back by a soldier.

"Free them!" yelled Thomas the Woodsman, and suddenly the crowd surged forward, but, like Robin's father, they were pushed back at sword point by a line of soldiers ringing the gallows.

"We've done nothing wrong!" shouted Marian, trying to rally the crowd.

"It's us today. It will be you tomorrow," cried Marian's mother. "Now is the time to rise up!"

Robin looked around desperately. If only he had

his bow and a quiver of arrows, he'd send the soldiers fleeing like rats before a flood. Or at least he'd shoot the hangman, a huge, barrel-chested man wearing a black hood. He had his hand on a lever that would spring the trapdoors and drop them to their deaths.

"Silence!" demanded the Sheriff, mounting the steps to the gallows. "The next man or woman who speaks will do so for the last time. My soldiers will see to it!"

For the moment the Sheriff's threat stunned the crowd into silence.

"The four prisoners you see before you have stolen and cheated and mocked my authority," said the Sheriff. "If it was only me they were mocking, I would not care, but I represent Good King Richard. And when they dishonor me, they dishonor the king. Therefore these four must die, as will anyone else who chooses to defy my authority."

"Please, spare my son!" cried the Earl of Locksley. "He's only a boy!"

"Father!" Robin called out.

The Sheriff turned to the soldiers standing behind him on the gallows. "Get on with it!" he hissed. "Quickly now, before we have a riot on our hands."

"Hear me, my friends! How much longer must we

stand by and allow the Sheriff to trample our rights?" shouted Marian as her head was being forced into one of the hangman's nooses. "The Sheriff has cheated the king of his taxes! Now he wants to cheat us too and drive us from our lands."

"I only do what the law prescribes," said the Sheriff.

"You mock the law," said Geoffrey. "You wish to hang me only because I often ruled against you in court."

"It's true!" someone yelled. "The magistrate's done nothing wrong."

"I have proof that the Sheriff has stolen from the king!" cried Marian. "Written in his own hand!"

"Silence!" thundered the Sheriff. His face was so red it looked as if it might burst into flames.

"His dungeon is filled with your neighbors," cried Marian's mother. "Mary! I saw your brother in there. Beth, your husband, Will, was imprisoned last summer. John, your son is not dead. He's—"

"Lies!" screamed the Sheriff, cutting her off.

"Not lies," said Marian. "Christopher, your father is wasting away in the dungeon even as I stand here."

"The babbling of a crazy young girl," snorted the Sheriff.

"Open your dungeon then!" yelled a woman in front.

"Release them!" shouted Thomas the Woodsman.

The crowd picked up the cry. "Release them! Release them! Release them!"

"There're hundreds of you!" shouted Marian. "Together you can accomplish anything! Whether we die or not this day isn't important. What matters is that you stand up to the Sheriff and take back your rights."

"Enough of this treasonous talk. Tighten the ropes!" cried the Sheriff. He had one eye on Marian and another on the crowd, which, inspired by Marian's words, seemed ready to attack.

The soldiers on the gallows pulled all the nooses tight, then stepped back.

Marian glanced down at the trapdoor beneath her feet, and her mouth went dry. She groaned and waited for the hangman to pull the lever, for the floor to go out from under her, and then for the rope to snap her neck.

CHAPTER SEVENTEEN

A GUEST AT THE HANGING

The Sheriff held out his hand as if to push back the crowd. "There's nothing you can do about it now!" he shouted. "The traitors will be hung!"

Marian shot a look at Robin. He looked back but didn't speak. He didn't need to. She knew what he was thinking: Two forever.

"My friends! There comes a time when we have to stand up for what is right and just," cried Marian, making a final, desperate plea. "You have the strength to do it. Come forward and declare that this evil must end, here and now!"

"She's right!" shouted Thomas.

"We've suffered long enough!" cried Mary.

"Rise up then!" shouted Marian. "Only you can free your loved ones who are dying in the dungeon."

The crowd roared and surged forward.

"Hold them back!" ordered the Sheriff. He swallowed nervously. "Do as I say!"

"In numbers there is strength!" shouted Marian. "There's no time to hesitate! Rise up!"

On Marian's command the people of Nottingham came forward with a tremendous roar. Three or four people, including Thomas the Woodsman and Anne the Seamstress, had boosted themselves onto the gallows. Anne caught the hangman's chin with her elbow and he went flying, releasing his grip on the lever. Within moments it was all over. The soldiers had been disarmed; the Sheriff, captured. Mercifully someone stepped forward and carefully slipped the noose off everyone's neck.

"You people won't get away with this!" thundered the Sheriff, trying to free himself. "When King Richard hears about this, he'll have you hung for treason."

"Oh, will he now?" came a deep voice from the edge of the crowd.

The man's voice held such calm authority that everyone turned.

"Who dares to speak for the king?" demanded the Sheriff.

"I do," came a deep, clear voice. A tall man in a long, hooded, brown cloak stepped forward. He pulled back the hood and a cascade of blond curls tumbled down around his shoulders.

The Sheriff paled. A murmur went through the crowd.

The man fixed his pale blue eyes on the Sheriff, then removed the rest of his cloak, revealing a purple coat with gold piping, leather breeches, and boots that shone like a new penny. He was the grandest person Marian had ever beheld.

"King Richard!" gasped the Sheriff. He shook off the hands of the crowd and bowed. "Your... Your Majesty," he stammered. "What an unexpected pleasure. If I'd known you were coming I would have prepared a feast."

"Prepared is not something I wanted you to be," said the king, striding up the stairs to the gallows. "That is why I came in disguise. I wanted to learn the truth without interference." He motioned to a young boy who hurried over with a sheet of parchment. "I received a most disturbing letter two days ago," he said, crossing the gallows. He handed the parchment to the Sheriff. "It alleges certain crimes committed by you against the citizens of Sherwood Forest."

The letter! Marian recognized it as the very one she'd placed in Bertram's saddlebag.

The Sheriff dismissed the letter with a wave of his hand. "The kingdom is full of malcontents. I can assure you there is no truth to these charges."

"Not so. They're all true," said Marian.

The king turned to face Marian, but the Sheriff quickly placed himself between the two. "Don't listen to her. She's a common thief," said the Sheriff.

"You're the thief!" shouted Marian. "And I can prove it too."

The king pushed the Sheriff aside and placed his hand on Marian's shoulder.

"Don't let Marian's age fool you," said the Sheriff. "Short snakes can be as deadly as long ones."

"Marian?" The king turned away from the Sheriff and addressed Marian. "Tell me, young maiden, are you the same Marian who wrote this letter?"

Marian swallowed. She had never spoken to a king before. "Yes, Your Majesty," she said. "I wrote that letter. And Robin, whose signature is beneath mine, is beside me."

The Sheriff sneered with contempt. "What can a

couple of thieves have to say that can be of any impor-
tance? We're wasting our time."

The king handed the Sheriff Marian's letter. "You
can read for yourself what can be so important."

"I can assure you, everything I wrote in my letter is
true," said Marian.

"Her word against mine," said the Sheriff. He
looked around nervously.

"Your Majesty, if you'll untie my hands, I'll give
you the proof I promised in the letter," said Marian.
"Please. I beg of you."

"Do it," ordered the king.

As soon as Marian's hands were free, she reached
into her secret pocket and drew out the folded papers.

"What have we here?" asked the king, taking the
papers.

When the Sheriff saw his records, his eyes got
round as gold pieces. "You…you stole those papers
from me!" he stammered.

"Perhaps," said Marian. "But was that worse than
what you stole from the king?"

"How dare you!" thundered the Sheriff. He
stomped his foot so hard the gallows quivered. "Do
you see what I mean, Your Majesty? These people have

no respect for the law."

King Richard wasn't listening to the Sheriff. He was too busy studying the records.

"It's a record of the taxes taken in," explained Marian. "It also shows how little of the money ever reached your court."

"Hold your tongue!" demanded the Sheriff.

"No, you hold yours," said the king sharply. He turned to his men. "Untie the prisoners and see that they are released." He waved the papers above his head and addressed the crowd. "This is all any court will need to convict the Sheriff many times over. As the girl has said, it's a clear record of his theft and deceit."

"Hail Good King Richard!" someone shouted from the crowd.

The Sheriff turned and tried to stifle the man with his gaze, but he was too late. The chant was quickly picked up by others, and in no time the square echoed with praises for Good King Richard.

"I believe you'll find the dungeon filled with many others wrongly condemned," said Marian. "The Sheriff held them there in secret so as to prevent a rebellion. I hope you can find a way to free them as well."

King Richard smiled down on Marian. "I'm sure I

can find a way," he said. "That's one of the privileges I have as king." He turned to the Sheriff. "Besides, I believe we will need to make room in that dungeon for a new resident."

"Your Majesty," said the Sheriff desperately. "Believe me, I never—"

"It is one thing to steal from me," interrupted King Richard, "but I will not tolerate the mistreatment of my subjects. Your days of cruelty and theft are over."

"But, Your Majesty—"

"Take him away!" ordered the king. "Off with him! To the dungeon!"

Two of the Sheriff's own soldiers quickly shackled the Sheriff by the hands. Then they led him kicking and screaming off the gallows and through the crowd, which showered him with taunts and curses all the way to the castle.

"I owe you and your friend Robin a debt of gratitude," said King Richard. He placed a hand on Marian's shoulder. "You are an exceptional young lady. Where did you ever learn how to read and write?"

"From my mother, sir," said Marian. "I hope you don't hold it against me."

"On the contrary," said the king. "We could use

more young ladies like you in the kingdom." He smiled at Robin. "And young men like you."

Marian held up two fingers and Robin touched them with his own. "Two forever," they said in unison.

The king wrapped his big arms around Robin and Marian and stepped to the edge of the gallows.

"These two courageous souls have made us all proud today," he announced. "In recognition of their courage and devotion to the crown, I'm awarding them both the royal medal of honor." The king then opened the bag hanging from his belt, reached in, and pulled out two badges, which he pinned on Marian and Robin.

Marian's jaw nearly dropped to the ground.

"We're honored, Your Majesty," said Robin, bowing.

"We'll serve you well," promised Marian.

"You already have," said the king, smiling. He then placed one hand on Marian's shoulder, the other on Robin's. "Long may you both live!"

"Hail Marian and Robin!" cried someone in the crowd.

Within moments everyone was shouting the praises of Marian, Robin, and the king. The Sheriff's festival had turned out to be better than anyone could have predicted. They hadn't gotten to see a hanging, but they'd gotten something even better, their freedom.

Marian beamed. She could not remember ever feeling quite so good, though a moment later she felt even better when she saw her father take her mother into his arms.

"I thought you were gone for good," said Marian's father.

"I had too much to live for," said Lady Eleanor. After a long embrace, she turned and took Marian by the hand, studied her for a moment, then swept her up into her arms and squeezed her close.

Marian shut her eyes and let out a sigh she'd been holding in for years. She had a mother again. She had a family again.

Even a certain piglet could have easily predicted it: They were going to be three forever, once again.

Girls to the Rescue

Edited by Bruce Lansky

A collection of 10 folk- and fairy tales featuring courageous, clever, and determined girls from around the world. When girls see this collection they will say, "Finally! We get to be the heroes." As Lansky brought nursery rhymes into the 1990s with his bestseller *The New Adventures of Mother Goose*, this groundbreaking book updates traditional fairy tales for girls aged 8-12.

Girls to the Rescue, Book #2

Edited by Bruce Lansky

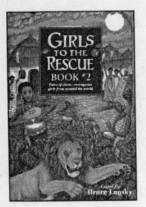

Here is the second groundbreaking collection of folktalkes featuring 10 clever and courageous girls from around the world. You will meet Jamila, a girl who saves her village from a terrible lion; Adrianna, a Mexican girl who rescues her family's farm from ruin; and Vassilisa, a Russian aristocrat who saves her brother from prison. (Ages 8-12)

"*Girls to the Rescue* turns a new page and Prince Charming is history."
—Sally Han, *New York Daily News*

Girls to the Rescue, Book #3

Edited by Bruce Lansky

The runaway success of the *Girls to the Rescue* series continues with this third collection of folktales from around the world, featuring such heroic girls as Emily, a girl who helps a runaway slave and her baby daughter reach safety and freedom; Sarah, a Polish girl who saves her father from prison; and Kamala, a Punjabi girl who outsmarts a pack of thieves. (Ages 8-12)

"Inspiring."
—Mary Hance, *Nashville Banner*

Throw a *Girls to the Rescue* Party!

We have created a *Girls to the Rescue* event kit that we make available to bookstores and schools. The kit includes fun activities, bookmarks, and buttons for all participants. If you want to have a *Girls to the Rescue* party, contact your local bookstore and ask them to set one up. And if you want to have a *Girls to the Rescue* party at school, have your teacher contact our Promotion Manager by using the address on the order form in the back of this book.

Perform a *Girls to the Rescue* Play!

Now you can produce *Girls to the Rescue* plays at school using scripts and materials from Baker Plays. Have your teacher contact Baker Plays at (617) 482-1280 for more information.

Real Girl Heroes Wanted!

Are you a clever, courageous hero? We're looking for stories about real-life heroic girls between the ages of seven and fourteen. Write your story in five hundred words or less, and you may be one of the twenty-five winners of $100. Send the story (preferably type-written) and a photograph of the young hero to: Heroic Girls Contest, Meadowbrook Press, 5451 Smetana Drive, Minnetonka, Minnesota, 55343. Contest limited to girls age fourteen and under. Winning heroes may also be featured in an upcoming book. (If you would like your photo returned, please include a self-addressed, stamped envelope.)

Free Stuff for Kids
1997 Edition

by the Free Stuff Editors

With over 4 million copies in print, this perennial children's favorite is "newer" than ever—over 90% of the offers in the '97 edition are brand new. And, *Free Stuff for Kids '97* will have more offers than ever before.

4,133,000 copies in print.
ISBN: 0-671-87288-5 **$5.00**

Hundreds of free and up-to-a-dollar things kids can send for by mail!

For a generation, kids have been sending away for the best free and up-to-a-dollar offers found in *Free Stuff for Kids*. Kids loved the book because of all the fun offers, plus the fact they could get great stuff through the mail. Parents knew the offers in the book were educational and fun. Teachers understood the book helped motivate children to practice their letter-writing skills.

Today's children do much of their writing at a computer keyboard and receive e-mail. *Free Stuff '97* remains pertinent to this new generation of children with all new offers of computer software. At the same time, it contains fun offers that will make children want to step away from their computer screens and learn about the real world around them. This year's edition also has offers that expands the age group that would be interested in *Free Stuff for Kids*.

- **A huge computer section, including many internet freebies**
- **Cool toys, crafts, and professional-sports fan packs**
- **More offers that promote books and reading**
- **Fun school supplies, like glow-in-the dark pencils**

Bruce Lansky's Poetry Party

by Bruce Lansky
Illustrated by Stephen Carpenter

The "King of Giggle Poetry" has put together an all-new collection with more laugh-out-loud poems than any other children's poetry book. *Poetry Party* contains the funniest poems about such subjects as parents who won't let their kids watch TV, yucky school lunches, and dogs that "water" the flowers. Hardcover.

Kids Pick the Funniest Poems

Selected by Bruce Lansky
Illustrated by Stephen Carpenter

The funniest poetry book for kids ever published, it includes hilarious verses by Dr. Seuss, Shel Silverstein, Judith Viorst, Jack Prelutsky, Jeff Moss, and others—all selected by a panel of 300 elementary-school kids. Carpenter's 75 irresistible line drawings add to the humor. Hardcover.

A Bad Case of the Giggles

Selected by Bruce Lansky
Illustrated by Stephen Carpenter

Bolt the doors and get out of earshot when kids discover this book…it will leave them with "a bad case of the giggles." It's jam-packed with poems about stinky feet, burps, and other topics kids find hilarious. The book contains poems by favorite poets: Shel Silverstein, Jack Prelutsky, Judith Viorst, and Jeff Moss. Hardcover.

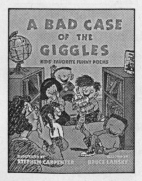

Order Form

Qty.	Title	Author	Order No.	Unit Cost (U.S. $)	Total
	Bad Case of the Giggles	Lansky, B.	2411	$15.00	
	Bruce Lansky's Poetry Party	Lansky, B.	2430	$12.00	
	Free Stuff for Kids	Free Stuff Editors	2190	$5.00	
	Girls to the Rescue	Lansky, B.	2215	$3.95	
	Girls to the Rescue, Book #2	Lansky, B.	2216	$3.95	
	Girls to the Rescue, Book #3	Lansky, B.	2219	$3.95	
	Kids Are Cookin'	Brown, K.	2440	$8.00	
	Kids Pick the Funniest Poems	Lansky, B.	2410	$15.00	
	Kids' Holiday Fun	Warner, P.	6000	$12.00	
	Kids' Party Games and Activities	Warner, P.	6095	$12.00	
	New Adventures of Mother Goose	Lansky, B.	2420	$15.00	
	Young Marian's Adventures	Mooser, S.	2218	$4.50	
				Subtotal	
			Shipping and Handling, see below		
			MN residents add 6.5% sales tax		
				Total	

YES, please send me the books indicated above. Add $2.00 shipping and handling for the first book and $.50 for each additional book. Add $2.50 to total for books shipped to Canada. Overseas postage will be billed. Allow up to four weeks for delivery. Send check or money order payable to Meadowbrook Press. No cash or C.O.D.'s please. Prices subject to change without notice. **Quantity discounts available upon request.**

Send book(s) to:

Name _____

Address _____

City _____ State _____ Zip _____

Telephone (_____) _____

Purchase order number (if necessary) _____

Payment via:

☐ Check or money order payable to Meadowbrook (No cash or C.O.D.'s please.)
   Amount enclosed $ _____

☐ Visa (for orders over $10.00 only)   ☐ MasterCard (for orders over $10.00 only)

Account #_____

Signature _____ Exp. Date _____

You can also phone us for orders of $10.00 or more at 1-800-338-2232.

A *FREE* Meadowbrook catalog is available upon request.

Mail to: Meadowbrook Press
5451 Smetana Drive, Minnetonka, MN 55343

Phone (612) 930-1100   Toll-Free 1-800-338-2232   Fax (612) 930-1940